GIRL CRAZY

GIRL CRAZY

COMING OUT EROTICA

EDITED BY

SACCHI GREEN

Published in the United States by
Cleis Press Inc., P.O. Box 14697, San Francisco, California 94114.

Printed in Canada.
Cover design: Scott Idleman
Text design: Frank Wiedemann
Cover photo: David Perry/Getty Images
Cleis Press logo art: Juana Alicia
First Edition.
10 9 8 7 6 5 4 3 2 1

ISBN 13: 978-1-57344-352-4

Contents

| INTRODUCTION

Girl Crazy! You know that feeling, whether you've come out to yourself, to your community or to the world. You know the surge of excitement flooding body and soul, the rush of pleasure and pain too intense to be denied, the certainty, at last, of who you are and who you want. From self-discovery to the first thrill of girl-on-girl erotic play, from the tender growth of lasting love to explorations of the fiercer shores of sex, these nineteen writers know the feeling, too, and share their no-holds-barred tales of the highs and lows and kinky twists of first times and coming out.

College kids acting out for *Girls Gone Wild* get even wilder once the cameraman has gone. A lonely businesswoman discovers how far her young chauffeur can drive her. Butch buddies find secret desires racing out of control. A summer job constructing wilderness trails sparks trailblazing into very different territory. Girls who thought they knew it all discover ways of getting down and dirty beyond their wildest dreams. These and a wide range of other intimate stories, some drawn from real-life experience, take you where you know you want to be—among girls who love girls who are girl crazy.

Sacchi Green
Amherst, Massachusetts

SPITTING SEEDS

Sommer Marsden

Erin had dark hair the color of chocolate, wide green eyes, and pale freckled cheeks. The summer of our first year of college, she wore a yellow bikini. Her body was more boyish than mine; where my hips flared, hers were tucked and muscular like a swimmer's. Where my breasts swelled, hers were small and compact. She barely filled out the sunshine-colored triangle cups of her bathing suit, a fact she moaned about constantly.

"Oh, to have tits like you, Rita."

"Don't say tits, it's rude." I couldn't help laughing, though. Erin was the only person who had ever made me laugh so hard I peed my pants. The fact that I peed my pants made her laugh harder. Which made me laugh harder. By the end of it all, my face ached, my stomach hurt, and my pants were wet.

"Tits, tits, tits," she chanted. She dragged her toes through the dark lake water as the float bounced on its tether.

"You are a heathen," I snorted. The sun was at its hottest,

but instead of being in the water, we sat on the float baking in the heat.

"I am hungry, is what I am. Did Jill and Lisa leave us any food?"

Jill and Lisa were working their summer jobs at the chicken stand. They did the day shift, Erin and I worked the evening shift. Low pay but free food, flexible schedules, tips, and time to hang at the lake, drive to the beach, and party: all you could ask of a summer job. It paid for the cabin and food and beer. Perfect.

"Sure. There's..."

"Don't say it!"

"Chicken!"

"And let me guess," Erin giggled. "Corn on the cob, slaw, hush puppies, and chocolate cake."

"You are psychic."

"Blech. Do we have anything besides food from work?"

"I think we have some Ramen noodles, old eggs, old milk, and a watermelon." I flicked my foot through the water, and a rain of drops came down on us. I shivered and Erin squawked.

"Ooh, I like watermelon. Come on," she said, and stood. The wooden float sloshed in the water, and I closed my eyes with the swaying motion. "I'm hungry. Bring those tits and let's eat."

"Your tits are fine," I grumbled, but I followed her. She skipped up the float toward the shore, her yellow bathing suit riding up to show a crescent of snow-white skin rimmed by tan. My stomach grumbled. I really was hungry.

"Where is it?" Erin called, running ahead.

"In the cooler on the sunporch!"

"Where'd we get it?" She had completely disappeared from view. I rolled my eyes. Why did she care?

"My mother! When she came to visit Tuesday she brought it.

She bought it from a roadside stand on the way up." I lowered my voice as I came into the cabin.

Erin plunked the huge melon on the counter and found our one cutting knife. She wielded it as if it were a machete and turned, grinning. "Careful, I'm starved. Don't piss me off."

"You're so scary," I said. Then, out of the blue, I added, "Let's call in sick tonight. Let's pop some popcorn, and the four of us can watch scary movies and eat popcorn and drink beer and just be stupid."

"We are always stupid," Erin said, and stabbed the melon dead center. It made a dull thunk, and she yanked the blade up and stabbed again. "But that sounds good. Let's do *Halloween.* Jamie Lee Curtis is so cool. Maybe follow with some *Friday the 13th*. You know, the classics."

"My god. Give me that, you butcher." I took the knife from her and inserted it into the dark green marbled skin. I put some pressure on the handle, and the melon split with a liquidy crack. It opened like a big green egg along the jagged line of her attack. "Not the prettiest job, but we still have all our fingers," I teased.

I cut a few slices as Erin pulled out the plates. "You ever kissed a girl before?" she asked.

I stopped for a moment, a little surprised by the question. "You mean *kissed* kissed or like I kiss my aunt Diana?"

"Of course I don't mean that. We have *all* done that. Our mothers, our sisters, grandmas, aunts. That's a given, Rits." She was the only one allowed to call me "Rits."

"Oh, so you mean like..."

"Sucking face. Frenching. Have you ever kissed a girl? Like you were going to end up fucking her."

I remember it so clearly. I opened my mouth, closed it, opened it again. I had been temporarily struck mute.

"Hmm. I will take that as a no, then." Erin laughed, and her green eyes flashed in the sunny cabin kitchen. She put raggedy slices of watermelon on her plate and slapped a few on mine. "Let's eat on the sunporch."

I followed silently and we sat on the picnic table bench. The picnic table was painted a faded, peeling red, and if you weren't careful it left splinters in your ass. The sunporch itself was nothing more than a poured concrete floor and three walls of screens. It looked out onto a thick, lush bit of woods. Jill's cat, Camel, loved to lie in the random patches of sun that dappled the floor.

I bit into the watermelon: crisp, cool flesh; slick, wet rind. How was it that a watermelon stayed chilled no matter what the weather? "Good."

"Thank your mom for me," she mumbled, gobbling up her first slice. "Ahh, I was starved."

"I see that."

Erin licked her lips—lips that were just a shade darker than the watermelon flesh. "Good stuff. You ever spit the seeds when you were a kid?"

I laughed. "You are fully aware of my athletic abilities."

Erin giggled. "You mean lack thereof."

"Exactly. But yeah. When we were kids, we spit them. We used to make bets and then spit them. Needless to say, I always lost. I was never close."

"Oh come on, that bad?"

"Okay," I said, nibbling the cool fruit and spitting the seed softly onto my paper plate, "to be fair I think I may have won once or twice. But it was purely by accident. The law of averages."

She nodded as if making a decision. Her face looked a bit too serious for our silly conversation. Somewhere a seagull let out a victorious cry. It had most likely liberated a tasty morsel from a tourist. I had once seen a gull take off with an entire paper cup of French fries from the chicken shack.

"Let's play," Erin said.

"Oh, come on, I just told you I suck!" I started to laugh, but something in her expression stifled the laugh in my throat. "For what?"

"A kiss. If I get it in that round rust stain, I get to kiss you. Anywhere I want. If you win, you get the same. Or you don't have to kiss me at all. You can get a pass."

My throat seemed to have closed on its own, and my mouth had dried up. Not because I was upset by the rules she had laid out, but because I wasn't. I had grown damp against the sun-dried cotton of my bathing suit bottom, and I shifted with the new, warm wetness there. I stared at the round rust stain on the concrete patio. It was the size of a gallon of paint, a perfect reddish circle to aim for. "Okay," I managed, but my voice was so weak, I was sure she couldn't hear me.

But she nodded and smiled. "Are you sure? Because I'm dead serious. I've been..."

She tapered off and I waited, the bugs in the woods singing a restless summer song. Finally, I broke. "You've been what?"

"I've been attracted to girls for a while now, and I've wanted to kiss you for even longer than that. But our friendship..."

I nodded. "Is the most important thing."

"But if I'm going to kiss a girl for the first time—or anything... else—I want it to be you, Rits."

I nodded again. I could live with that. I could more than live with that. My nipples pressed against my bathing suit and I knew there was no hiding my arousal. "Okay. First one to hit the circle gets to kiss. Anywhere she wants."

Erin was more athletic than me. And patient. She would wait

to line up a shot, be it basketball or tennis or spitting seeds. Her first try and the shiny black seed bounced into the circle. It landed almost dead center.

"Just on the lips the first time," she said. Her lips were warm and soft and tasted of the fruit we had devoured. Erin stroked her tongue over mine softly until a needy little sound slid from my throat. A starburst of excitement and desire warmed my belly. She broke the kiss and touched my bottom lip with her sticky finger. "That was nice."

I missed on my first try, and felt a surprising disappointment. I clenched my fists when it was her turn, silently rooting for a hit. She did. The second shiny black seed bounced in next to the first.

Without a word, she untied the strings at the nape of my neck and my bikini top dropped, the ties tickling my upper thighs. The sun-bleached blonde hairs there rose with excitement. I noticed them and thought vaguely how lazy I was to only shave my legs up to the knee because my hair was blonde. When her lips touched my nipple, I sucked in a great breath of air and my skin broke out in a rash of goose bumps. "Oh, god," I said—clichéd, but completely honest.

Erin sucked my nipple into her hot little mouth, and an invisible line tugged from my breast to my pussy, pleasure so intense it almost hurt. Another hot flood of moisture escaped my body, and I felt a tickle in the back of my throat. I touched her dark hair and held her to my breast. She broke free, licking a path to my other nipple as my body's signals went haywire and I felt a deep chill despite the hot day. She traced one finger over the slit of my sex through my bikini bottom before pulling away.

"No cheating," she said, clearing her throat. Her voice had grown husky, and her eyes were shiny and slightly dazed.

It was my turn. I missed again, and frustration welled up in me. I bit my lip to keep from cussing. I would get my seed into the circle. Eventually.

"Don't worry, Rits. You'll do it," Erin said, reading my mind. She patted my leg, and I forgot all about my inept athletic skills. All I wanted was her mouth on me. There. She took another bite of melon and I watched the slick pink flesh disappear behind her full lips. I had to close my eyes to keep myself under control.

She screwed up her mouth like she was about to blow up a balloon and then let loose with a great whoop of air. The seed flew through the air as if in slow motion. It hit the dirty concrete two inches shy, bounced and landed on the very rim of the rusty red circle. I stopped breathing. Was it in? Was it out?

"You rule. You be the judge," Erin said. Her green eyes had turned a bit blue. Something they did when she was feeling intense.

"It's in," I said without hesitation. I watched her hands, a bit smaller than mine, tug at my pink bikini bottom; saw the contrast of her nut-brown fingers against the screaming hot-pink fabric.

"Lift up," she muttered, and I hiked my hips up off the scratchy picnic table bench. She kissed up my thighs and I watched, fascinated. I watched her lips on my leg, watched the tip of her ripe pink tongue dart out and leave a shiny wet trail on my skin; watched as her lips brushed the very tops of my thighs and watched as her tongue found me and worked me wide open. The sight of her tongue on my clit registered before the sensation. But when the sensation hit, it was sweet like sugar.

"Baby," I said. I had never called a woman that, and it felt perfectly natural. "Right—"

"Shhh," she said, and the vibration of her soft sound soaked into me so swiftly it stole my breath. Already I hovered right on the edge of coming, right on that velvet razor's edge. Her fingers splayed across my thighs, warming my skin. I silently prayed—prayed for her fingers inside of me. But I pressed my lips tight together and bit my tongue a little because her soft "shh" had been her way of asking that I let her be the guide. So I would.

Erin slid her rigid tongue past my clit and worked lower. I missed the intense pleasure of her wet pressure on my clit, but when she worked her tongue deep inside of me and my body pulsed around it, I sighed. She touched my waist, my belly, my nipples, and my whole body responded to the alternating touches: gentle then harsh, back and forth, so I never felt stable. I arched my hips up, not thinking, just moving against her—and then she pinned me down. Her forearm, looking so thin, but so strong, held me fast. And then her fingers did find me, and my eyelids slammed closed, and I was lost in the feel of her.

There was just the feel of her slippery tongue on my clit, her long fingers in my cunt, her soft hair on my thigh. The sunroom was lit up with afternoon yellow, and I felt the warm rays on my skin. I could hear the gulls and her wet ministrations as I came, and she laughed softly against my skin and then made me come again. The second time, my orgasm was less intense but beautifully lazy. I felt heavy and slow even as the heat of the day started to break a bit.

When it was finally my turn, when I finally landed a seed in the circle, her skin tasted like watermelon juice. Her pussy smelled like suntan oil and sweat and excitement. She was slightly sweet and musky on my tongue, the taste of her unique and unforgettable. When she came around my fingers, I had never been more pleased to evoke an orgasm.

We had several more seed-spitting contests that summer. We remained lovers for over two years before she left for college on the West Coast. Our friendship never wavered, was never even in danger of weakening. And to this day, when I taste watermelon, I smell warm girl skin and hear seagulls. I think of sunshine yellow bikinis, and orgasms.

BECOMING WILD

Kyle Sontz

Okay, so it was Spring Break, right? My boyfriend, Jake, had to stay at the University of Michigan 'cause he had to practice. He was the pitcher for the baseball team. So it was just me and my three best girlfriends, partying in Cancun with MTV. This one night we were way drunk off of margaritas, and these guys with cameras came up to us and asked if we wanted to be on *Girls Gone Wild.*

Like I said, it was Spring Break, and we were all totally drunk and feeling really hot dressed in little bikini tops and sarongs, and we had been dieting all winter to make sure we looked perfect. Beth and Lindsey both flashed the camera, whooping and playing with themselves. I felt like doing something totally crazy, totally unexpected, and Lynne had just gotten her nipples pierced so she couldn't show off her tits. When the cameraman winked and trained the lens on me, I grabbed Lynne and started kissing her. Somewhere in the back of my mind I knew the camera guys were cheering us on and my friends were screaming along with the general roar of the crowd, but in that moment all I was aware of were her lips on mine, my hand twined in her long red hair.

The next morning—okay, afternoon—we woke up nursing awful hangovers. Lynne stayed in bed with the covers pulled over her head, so it was just three of us who staggered down to the hotel restaurant.

None of us felt like talking much as we sipped our Bloody Marys, but by the time the waiter came with our plates of eggs and toast, Lindsey and Beth had recovered enough to start rehashing the previous night.

"Omigod," moaned Beth. "I can't believe my boobs are gonna be on, like, *Girls Gone Wild Volume 37*. I'll be soooo embarrassed if anyone at school sees it. Now I'll never have a boyfriend again!"

"Don't be stupid, you ho!" said Lindsey. "Guys are gonna be, like, all over you now! But like, what if they put us on those commercials? My dad totally watches those, what if he sees me?"

"Oh come on, like your dad's gonna be looking at your face."

"Ew, you're so fucking gross!" Lindsay threw a breadstick at Beth, who ducked and started giggling madly.

I had stayed quiet, chewing on my omelet, hoping they would be too distracted by their own problems to remember mine. No such luck.

"Omigod, Amy, what *was* that last night?"

"What was what?" I mumbled through a mouthful of egg. "I was, like, so drunk I don't even remember." My eyes stayed trained on my plate.

"You, like, totally made out with Lynne! It was crazy! Everyone at school's gonna start saying you're a lesbian!"

"Don't be stupid, I've been dating Jake for, like, a year. I'm *so* not a lezzie. I mean, girls always make out with each other on those videos, you've seen it! Boys totally love it when we do that. It was all just for fun."

"Yeah, but, like, when other girls do it? It looks, like, fake. Like they don't really want to. You and Lynne, though, were totally going at it! I mean, you kept going even after the camera guys were done. What was up with that?"

I shrugged and filled my mouth with toast. "Still don't remember," I maintained, spraying crumbs everywhere. "Like I said, I was way trashed."

Finally they dropped the subject, and when we went back up to the room, Lynne didn't bring it up either. I didn't know if she actually had been too drunk to remember, or if she was really embarrassed and didn't want to talk about it, but she didn't act like anything had happened.

I couldn't forget, though. The rest of the week was a blur. I probably looked normal on the outside, drinking and partying and flirting with boys like always, but on the inside I was still in that one bar, my arms around Lynne and my mouth pressed against hers. Once or twice I caught myself staring at her, remembering what she smelled like.

I didn't know what to make of it. I couldn't be gay, I had a boyfriend! Lynne and I had been friends since the first day of freshman year. And yeah, I always thought she was really hot, and fun to be around. I was closer with her than I was with Beth and Lindsey, but it wasn't like I had a crush on her or anything. And besides, I liked skirts and makeup and stuff. Didn't lesbians have to play with trucks when they were little, and wear boy's clothes and have short hair? I didn't do anything like that. And, I mean, I was so fucking drunk. I knew once I got home and saw my boyfriend I'd be back to normal.

Jake was really sweet, too. He met me at the airport with a dozen red roses! He took me straight to the fanciest restaurant in town, with tablecloths and candles and everything. He had made reservations, and got champagne, and just treated me like a princess. I told him all about my trip, except for that one part, of course. I knew he'd probably think it was really hot—he'd actually asked me if I'd be willing to do a threesome sometime. But I just didn't want to tell him about it, it seemed too private. Still, dinner was really nice.

After dessert he drove me back to his apartment. We went into his bedroom and started to make love. Usually he wasn't that big into foreplay, but I guess he figured that tonight I should get a little extra. He started playing with my nipples until I was moaning. Then he slid his fingers under my thong and started finger-banging me. After a few minutes I started pushing against them, trying to show him where my clit was, but he thought that meant I was about to come so he took them away and got out of his pants. He asked me to go down on him. I didn't mind, so I went to work, licking and sucking and not really thinking about anything at all except how much unpacking I had to do the next day. Luckily it was a Saturday, and classes didn't start till Monday.

Once his dick was hard, he laid me down on the bed and got between my knees. When he started humping away, I made the expected sounds, gasping and saying "Oh yeah, just like that." Then, out of nowhere, I started thinking about Lynne: the way her lips tasted, how soft the skin of her back was under my hands, how she shivered when I just barely grazed her breast. I tried to wrench my mind away, but suddenly everything Jake was doing to me felt a little better. In my mind his broad back and narrow hips became her soft curves. I imagined that each thrust of his dick was a penetration by her warm hand, and

I moaned louder. The sound must have excited him, because he started pumping even harder into me, jarring me out of my reverie. Before I could get the sensation back, he shuddered and came into the condom I made him wear.

He lay heavily on me for a minute, then kissed me and heaved himself off. He rested one hand on my tit.

"How was it, babe?" He always asked, and my answer was always the same.

"Really good, baby." This time it was almost true. Usually after sex I'd spend the night at his place, but once he started yawning I rolled off the bed and started getting my clothes.

"Hey, where you going?"

"I've just had a really long flight, spent the whole week sleeping in the same room as three other girls. I need a night alone, is all. Tonight was great though, sweetie, really."

"Aw, okay. You want me to drive you home?"

I shook my head. "It's fine, the bus is right outside. You go to sleep."

"See you soon, babe. Love ya."

"Sweet dreams."

I went back to my dorm and pulled out my vibrator. That little battery-powered lifesaver was why it didn't bother me that Jake could never give me an orgasm. I got plenty on my own. I switched it on and held it between my legs, and unbidden, Lynne came floating into my mind again. I turned it off quickly, suddenly scared. First I couldn't get her out of my head during break, then she popped up while I was fucking Jake, and then again while I was trying to get myself off? What did it mean? Was I actually gay? I dropped the vibrator back in my sock drawer, grabbed my teddy bear, and tried to fall asleep. When I woke up to my alarm the next morning, I couldn't remember what I had dreamed about, except that whatever it was had made me feel warm and safe.

The four of us had all picked the same major, so it was no surprise to walk into my first-period communications class and see Lynne sitting there. Still, I felt my breath catch in my throat, and my heart pounded rapidly as I dropped my book bag onto the chair next to hers.

"Hey," she said, tucking a fiery curl behind her ear.

"How's it going?" I asked, praying that the heat I felt rising in my face wasn't a visible blush.

"Ugh, I can't believe the year's almost over! We're going to be seniors!"

"I know, crazy, right? Seems like just yesterday you and me and Beth and Lindsay met at freshman orientation. Where'd all that time go?"

Lynne smiled. "It's been great, though. I had a lot of fun in Cancun with you girls. I really feel like we all got even closer."

"Me too." I wondered if she remembered, if she had been thinking about it. Before I could work up the nerve to ask, we heard Beth and Lindsey from all the way down the hall, arguing about the ethics of not telling your fuckbuddy about your boyfriend and vice versa. They distracted us until the start of class.

"Finals are coming up," the professor reminded us at the end of class. "In order to make sure you are all adequately prepared, I want you to form small study groups and turn in weekly reports on the readings. The first assignment is due Thursday."

The whole class groaned. It wouldn't be so bad for the four of us, though, since we'd work together. It was always more fun that way. We set the next night as our first study date, and decided to meet in Lynne's room since it was closest to the center of campus.

I spent the next day on pins and needles. It took an hour to find just the right outfit, but I finally decided on my Seven jeans and a light pink tank top. I put on just a little makeup, some lip gloss, and mascara, and as I was combing my hair I caught a glimpse of myself in the mirror. It looked like I was getting ready for a first date with some cute boy.

I dropped the hairbrush and looked at my reflection. "Stop it," I told myself firmly. "Lynne is just your friend. This is not a date. She doesn't even like girls, and neither do you. Okay? Okay."

I looked sternly into my eyes, trying to make myself believe it, and then grabbed my purse and book bag and headed to Lynne's room.

Surprise, surprise, Beth and Lindsay hadn't shown up yet. I perched on Lynne's desk and tried to make small talk while she straightened up her room. I told her about my date with Jake.

"And then after dessert he took me back to his room. It was really sweet."

"Yeah? Did he make you come this time?"

I blushed. When Jake and I started dating, I mentioned to the girls that he sometimes didn't let me finish, so now every time I mentioned us making love they asked me if I got to come. I usually giggled and lied and talked about how great he was now, how many little tricks he knew, but tonight I didn't feel like keeping up the charade.

"Of course not. He never does, why would he change now?"

"Wait, he's never made you come before?"

I blushed and just shook my head.

"But he's not the first guy you've hooked up with, right?"

"Nah. Freshman and sophomore year I went home with a few frat guys. Had a boyfriend in high school, we had sex in the backseat of his car."

"Okay, but were any of them any good?"

I started to get annoyed. What was she, a sex therapist or

something? "I mean, sure, I guess. Sex is always nice, it's not a big deal if they make me come or not."

"Sweetie, sex isn't supposed to be 'nice.' You mean to say none of those boys has ever made your toes curl?" She walked over so she was standing in front of me. I started to tremble slightly.

"No, but, I mean, so what? I've got my vibrator. And it's not like it matters that much. I don't really mind. So long as they're happy, you know?"

Lynne put one hand on each of my knees and spread them apart. She stepped closer to me, so that my knees were pressing against either side of her waist. "But Amy, what makes *you* happy?" She leaned in and just barely grazed her lips against mine.

I responded without thinking, gently at first, but when her tongue snuck into my mouth, I pulled back.

"Wait, but...what is...are you...?"

"I've known who I am since I was fourteen. Fell for you the first day of freshman year, but figured it'd wreck our friendship if I said anything. But over break...well, you don't kiss like a straight girl, that's all I have to say. And I saw how you looked at me after. Knew there was something inside you that you just couldn't admit to yet."

"But I'm not a—"

She cut me off. "It doesn't matter what you call yourself, straight, bisexual, femme, whatever. All that matters is that you want this, and so do I." She started kissing me again, one hand on my waist, the other playing gently with my nipple. I couldn't resist and started kissing her harder, pulling her close to me. A sudden concern pierced my excitement.

"But wait, Lindsay and Beth are coming over to study! What if they...?"

"Don't worry about them. I told them I was sick and had to reschedule for tomorrow. We've got all night to ourselves." With that she took me by the hand and pulled me off the desk, our mouths meeting again in earnest.

We somehow made it to her bed without separating our lips. She peeled off my tank top, and I slowly unbuttoned her shirt, revealing her pale breasts. She tugged off my jeans, and I slid my hands down her hips, removing her skirt. As she knelt there, almost naked, I couldn't keep myself from grinning. My face must have mirrored hers.

She reached around to unhook my bra. I giggled. "You're much faster at that than any of my boyfriends have been."

Lynne smiled. "Well, you know, I wear them too."

"You're not wearing one tonight," I retorted.

She shrugged. "Figured I'd make it that much easier for you."

"This is the easiest decision I've ever made," I whispered. I pushed her down and pulled her panties down her thighs. I wanted to go down on her, taste her, make her feel as good as I always wished I could feel. I gently nosed apart her pink lips and inhaled her scent, rich and tangy. It was my first time going down on a girl, but I knew exactly how to do it—all I had to do was exactly what I'd always wanted.

I started licking her gently, just barely pressing against her inner lips, up and around her clit hood. My hands crept gently up her belly, stroking her, and I grew light-headed from the sensation of her soft skin responding to my touch. She started to shiver as my tongue played around her clit, never touching the sensitive tip directly. She started to give me a little more guidance, pressing her flesh against my lips, showing me exactly how to touch her.

I couldn't believe that I had to beg my boyfriends for five

minutes of oral sex. I never wanted to stop. Lynne was getting wetter and wetter, and her clit had swollen so much that every lick seemed to be bringing her closer to orgasm. I experimented with everything I thought would feel good: circling, figure eights, licking straight up and down and side to side. I put my mouth around her clit, breathed hot air on it, sucked it gently like it was a tiny cock. She loved having my whole mouth cover her, so I started eating her in earnest, lapping like she was a girl-flavored ice-cream cone.

"Oh, yes, please, more!" she started to cry. "I'm so close...I'm going to come!" I kept my face down there while she bucked and writhed, letting her guide the action so that her orgasm was long and hard. When it was over she flopped back down, breathing heavily, and as I looked up I saw that her breasts and stomach were coated with a delicate sheen of sweat.

"Pretty good for a straight girl," she said when she had caught her breath.

"I thought you said it didn't matter if I was straight or not."

"Mmm. Sure doesn't." With that she pulled me up close to her and kissed me deeply, my whole face still sticky with her juices. As we were kissing she lay back down, positioning me so I was on my hands and knees over her. Her mouth made its way to my breast, and I shuddered and moaned as she sucked on it hard, nibbling gently. One of her hands snuck up in between my legs, and I cried out.

"Feel good?" she murmured.

"Is this how sex is supposed to be?" I asked.

She didn't answer, just looked into my eyes. Whatever this was, it sure didn't feel "nice." I moaned and rocked my hips against her hand. This felt even better than my vibrator. It was like she knew just how my body worked, just how to make everything feel perfect. I almost started to cry from pleasure. I spread my knees even wider apart, moved closer down, closer to her body. Her hand was strong and sure, she just kept stroking and caressing and circling me, and I knew she wouldn't stop until I came. Her whole attention was focused on my body and its responses, and I let myself go, tossing my hair, crying out, letting her see on my face just how good she was making me feel.

I wanted the feeling to last forever, but finally I just couldn't take it. "Oh, god, Lynne, I'm about to come...please don't stop, please, please, please!"

"I'd never stop," she whispered, and at that I exploded, bucking so hard the bed shook, and I came into her hand. I ground down until I trapped her wrist in between our bodies, making her laugh. When I couldn't come anymore, I flopped at her side, one leg stretched across her lean flanks, and kissed her cheek.

"So that's what it's like when girls really go wild, isn't it?"

She laughed. "Those poor boys have no idea what really happens when the cameras leave."

ROAD TRIP

Kirsten Monroe

We decided to shave our armpits for our Saturday afternoon outing to the bar. Don't ask me why. It's not like we cared about impressing any coworkers who might show up, or any of the locals either—a bunch of aging, nicotine-stained biker dudes and babes. The Long Spur was the only bar within fifty miles, and it wasn't much, but it wasn't nothing, either, and cleaning up seemed like the prudent thing to do.

We'd been busting our asses for three weeks straight building trails across Idaho, our post–college graduation gig. We earned two days off to scrub off the dirt and down some beer. Come Monday morning, we'd be back on the line. That morning we arrived back at the bunkhouse all strung out, mosquito bit, and so ready for beer and loud music that we could have screamed.

So Millie and I shaved ourselves up, washed off the grit, and hit the road, radio blaring, armpits tingling, ready for anything.

We'd been smoking some weed scored from a local guy on the crew who had this stash in his trailer that looked like a bale of hay, all rough and stems, but so sweet and fresh that just smelling it made you feel like you were floating on a cloud.

We flew out of the bunkhouse with a six-pack for good measure, playfully racing each other to my beat-up Pinto. It was good to be alive. We were feeling fine, maybe too fine, and about halfway to the Long Spur, we got lost. The funniest part was, to get to the Long Spur from the Forest Service bunkhouse you didn't have to take any turns at all. Turn left out of the driveway, head down the road for fifteen miles, and you're there, big old neon Budweiser sign bringing you right in for an easy landing. How we got lost, I couldn't tell you, but there we were, all cleaned up with our slick, sweet-smelling pits, and going in circles. I kept turning around in driveways, laughing my ass off, as if getting lost was the funniest thing ever.

Millie wasn't much help. She made me pull over so she could look at the bark of a big oak tree. "Oh my god, Bryn," she yelled, feigning panic. "Pull over! I don't think that tree is real. I have to touch it." She walked around and around that damn tree, fondling its bark.

"Jesus, of course it's a real tree," I yelled at her. "If it isn't real, it wouldn't be breathing and I can see it breathing." That put us on the ground in a spasm of laughter. It took Millie forever to let go of that tree. She knelt to the ground and gazed lovingly at the "oak nuts" that had fallen around it. After an eternity of discussing the botanical wonders of the oak nut, we finally remembered they're called acorns, and that was even funnier than going in circles.

We finally got back in the car and had ourselves pretty well straightened out when a huge eight-point buck leaped out of the woods, all legs and hooves and horns, nearly hitting us head-on and causing me to brake hard, sending the car skidding sideways.

By some miracle, we missed the lucky bastard. He shook his

rack and took one long look back at us before bounding off into the woods. We pulled slowly to the side of the road and just sat there.

"Damn, that was close," I said, my hands shaking. Millie sat for a long time with her head in her hands, bouncing her knees up and down. "Fuck the bar—let's just stay here and get a grip. The beer is behind the seat."

We gathered up the toppled but unbroken bottles and stumbled through the thick, cool woods. We found a small, sunny clearing in the middle of a cedar grove. I twisted open a couple of beers and sank into the dampish meadow grass, propping my head up on one of Millie's crossed thighs.

"How did we miss that fucking deer?" Millie asked. She sucked down several gulps of beer before exclaiming, "Dammit, I'm horny."

She was too much.

"I'm serious. I'm horny, Bryn. I need to get laid. Right now. Fuck! It could always be the last time. Think about that!"

I giggled, still a little high and a little scared from the near miss. "That would suck indeed, but I don't think we'll be getting a whole lot of action out here in the middle of nowhere."

She took me by my shoulders, flipped me over like I was a naughty kid, and slapped me on the ass. "You're it."

"Yeah right, you stoned crazy bitch! You're whacked. What are you going to do, fuck me up the butt with a pinecone?"

"Don't be such a prude. Come on, strip. It'll be fun. What's not to love about fucking in wide open spaces with the wind whistling Dixie between your legs? Dare ya. Double-dog dare ya. Pussy. You're not really so tough, are you? Scaredy cat."

She wouldn't quit. She plucked a purple cornflower and twirled it in her fingers. She ran it along my cheek, across my chest, and down one leg.

"We're young. We're alive. We're single. There's absolutely no fucking reason why we shouldn't." Millie smiled at me and raised her hands and shoulders into a question. "Give me one reason why not."

I could hear the sound of a woodpecker pounding holes in a nearby snag.

I realized at that moment that Millie, in all of her free-spirited hilarity, was serious about the fucking. Why did she have to dare me? She shook out her ponytail, long wavy blonde hair falling across her shoulders. She slipped out of her tank top and stood up braless in her faded jeans, spinning around, following her young, firm breasts in circles, the filtered sunlight giving her muscular body an unearthly glow.

She took my hand and pulled me up off the ground, grabbing my ass as I stood up. She pressed her face to my neck and nibbled at my ear, and then reached into my shirt and pinched a nipple hard.

"Ouch, Millie! That hurt."

I felt myself getting wet.

She giggled and put her hands on her hips. "You need to lighten up, Bryn. Slam another beer. Let's have some fun."

"You're serious, aren't you? I might. Maybe."

Millie raised her arms in the air and howled like a wolf.

"Shhhh! Who knows who might come driving along here? You're so out of control."

She pulled off my T-shirt and signaled me to follow her to a cedar tree with low, thick branches. She grinned like a little girl and scaled up a few levels, settling herself on a thick branch that made her look like she was straddling a giant bark-covered cock.

"Damn, Millie, you are like a fucking forest nympho," I said. I followed her up to the dick branch and situated myself behind her, cedar boughs grazing my back. The sweet smell of that oxygen-exhaling tree's breath swirled around us as we parted our legs across its bark. My breasts pressed against Millie's long hair and her smooth, strong shoulder blades as I steadied myself against her.

"Touch me Bryn, come on. This living, breathing tree loves me. You know you want to love me too."

I pulled her hair to one side, wrapped my arms around her waist, and tentatively kissed her shoulder. Her skin radiated lust. She reached back and ran her hands down my thighs, tilted her head back, and inhaled deeply.

"Good girl. Now touch me here."

Millie unzipped her jeans and took my hand, guiding it down to her cunt, already swollen and wet. I could feel the heat rippling across her skin.

"And here."

She pulled my fingers to her clit. I imagined pleasuring myself while I fingered her, letting her moans guide my strokes. Maybe it was the pot, but her clit felt huge beneath my fingertips. It was, I admit, intoxicating. Okay, it was more than intoxicating. It was fucking amazing and incredibly freeing. I began to lose myself in sensation and pleasure. I continued rubbing her dripping pussy and leaned against her back, my free hand stroking her hardened nipples.

Millie literally squealed with pleasure, a high girlish sound I'd never heard her make. There was nothing high-pitched about Millie, but there she was, perched in a tree, me fucking her with my fingertips, and her squealing silver bells of joy like a woodland fairy.

"Bryn," Millie said, placing her hand atop mine. "Let's go back to the meadow."

We climbed down like a couple of jungle Janes. Millie skipped back to the meadow, breasts bouncing, arms outstretched, singing some old folk song while I trotted after her, only half-believing what was happening, the craziness of it, the beauty of it, the thrill of it—and only half-believing that I would be brave enough to let go completely.

I let Millie pull me down on top of her in the grass. She was all smiles and giggles, obviously thrilled to have lived to fuck again. I straddled her and took one of her hard nipples in my mouth. I sucked at it awkwardly and bit down, tugging on it and letting it pop out of my mouth with drama, masking my nervousness with bravado.

God she smelled good, like soap and ferns and weed. She turned me over and slid down my body, my stomach slick with sweat and dew. She spread my legs and licked my thighs. Her tongue traced an arc across my buttocks and into my cunt with gentle urgency. She buried her face deep in my understory and licked me hard and fast, her hands under my ass, pushing my crotch skyward.

She thrust her tongue in deep, and then singed a trail of fire around my swollen clit, her fingers butterfly wings of pleasure that stripped me of all inhibition. She moved her hands, wet with my juices, up my sides and onto my tits, rubbing my aching nipples. My hips twisted uncontrollably beneath her. She slid up my wet stomach, squeezing my breasts together and putting both throbbing nipples into her mouth at once, making little circles with her tongue and biting just enough to make me go crazy. Pleasure and pain shot through my body, and I wrapped my legs around her waist, the universe expanding in a ball of red-hot flame. She took a fistful of my hair and pulled my neck sideways, licking my throat and breasts. I shuddered and moaned with pleasure.

Then she reversed position and went down on me again, her

dewy blossom a wildflower hovering above my face. I licked at it lightly at first, then pulled her hips down, wanting to explore deeper, her juices wetting my lips while I enjoyed her animal taste.

I explored the inner edges of her petals with my tongue, sliding my fingers carefully into her labyrinth. Millie's clit pulsed in my mouth, quivering like forbidden fruit. Mesmerized, I wrapped my tongue around it again and again, a moth to a flame. She moaned with pleasure, her hips grinding, her breasts against my hips, her long hair draped across my thighs, her tongue dancing around inside of me.

Millie lightly sucked my clit into her lips and held me there, aching, as she pushed her fingers in deep.

"Fuck me, Millie," I moaned, my voice deep and breathless, released, freed by the wings of lust. "You feel so good, Millie, God, your tongue. Mmmm, you are sunshine and earth and clouds and trees. Oh my god, Millie!" Millie's fingertips flickered across my G-spot, her lips pulsing against me as I arched my back and gave in to desire. She came moments later, a flood of hot come, ocean and sky, filling my mouth.

We lay there entwined in the grass, panting and giggling, and somehow it all seemed as natural as if we were Greek dryads come to life.

The sound of footsteps at the edge of the forest startled us to our feet.

We stood there in the meadow, sweaty and wet, pine needles and bits of moss and grass clinging to our skin. A light breeze stirred the trees. From behind a tall cedar emerged the buck, looking across the meadow at us with those big animal eyes, just watching, waiting to see what we'd do next.

DINNER AT CROMPTON'S

Scarlett French

I want to take you out for dinner," said Zoe, sounding determined.

"But..." I began, then faltered. Zoe was one of my favorite people, but things had been uncomfortable since she'd told me about her feelings. I held the receiver to my ear and struggled for the right words. She broke the silence.

"Look, I want to take you out for dinner—as friends—to say it's cool, okay? To set things straight and start over. There's no reason for this weirdness. So I fancy you. Big deal. You're not the only friend I fancy. It was worth a shot, but it shouldn't cost a friendship, should it?"

She was right, of course. "Okay, it's just that I felt bad. I didn't want to hurt you."

"Honey," she said, "I ain't hurtin', okay?"

"Okay," I said, feeling more relaxed. "I've missed you lately, you know. I haven't had anyone to be sarcastic with these last couple of weeks." I tried to sound breezy, but also, it was the truth. She had a wonderfully dry wit, and we set each other off. I had missed her company, her strength and humor.

"Good, I'm glad I'm hard to replace! All right then, I'll pick you up at eight tomorrow night," she said with a lilt in her voice, obviously pleased.

I sat down with the phone in my hand and thought about how the whole thing had transpired. We'd met for one of our usual coffees in the sun one Sunday, and, while walking along the bay, she'd turned to me with the coolest line I'd ever heard: "You know how you sat on my lap at Kirsty's party and sort of wriggled around? How would you like to do that naked?" I remember I'd been completely taken aback—I had sat on her lap at the party, but I hadn't meant anything by it. I'd never thought of Zoe that way, strangely perhaps, considering we talked about sex all the time and clearly had similar ideas on the matter. I remember she'd turned to me as I stood there unsure of what to say, and planted her mouth on mine, plunging her tongue straight in. I had automatically kissed her back before pulling away in confusion. Since then, I must admit, I had been thinking about that kiss. Well, not just the kiss, but also her tongue. It was kind of crimped around the edge, and I had since wondered how it might feel to be licked by such a tongue. Also, the force with which she kissed me...it does make you wonder how someone might be in bed, that's all. But I was happy with our friendship the way it was. I looked forward to hanging out together again, just like before her confession.

The following evening I took a long bath and clipped my nails. They needed doing anyway, and since I'd just had a bath, they were softened and easy to cut. I pulled on some jeans and a new top made from sari fabric. It was a nice warm night, so it was a good opportunity to wear it. Zoe turned up around seven-thirty with a smile on her face. A tall Greek woman with a great figure, Zoe suited figure-hugging clothes and tended to wear a lot of black, which made her look catlike. Tonight was no exception: she wore one of her usual ensembles, black T-shirt and black leather trousers. She loved those leather trousers and wore them even in the heat of summer.

She handed me a plastic container. "These are from my mum," she said. Inside were three varieties of homemade cookie; two kinds of spiced and a honey shortbread. "She said you must eat them all. She says all my friends and I are too thin."

We laughed then. "I can imagine her saying that!" I admired the way Zoe's mother pretended that her daughter was just falling behind a bit in the husband search and was so kind to us, when she had to know we were a bunch of dykes.

"That's so sweet of her, Zoe. Please tell her thank you from me and I promise to eat them all." I intended to anyway, as they were the best cookies around. I left them in my room to keep them away from my housemates.

We got into Zoe's car, and she started the engine.

"So, where are you taking me?" I asked her.

"Oh, it's just this little place," she said mysteriously as we pulled away from the curb. She obviously had a surprise in store, so I didn't press her. As we approached Oriental Bay, I figured she must be taking me to that popular new restaurant on the seafront, but we drove on past. The next street over we pulled into a hotel parking lot.

"Are we walking from here?" I asked.

"No, we're here," said Zoe. I looked at her quizzically. She pulled the keys from the ignition. "The restaurant here is apparently renowned for its vegetarian menu," she said, as she grabbed her bag and opened the car door.

We entered the hotel and headed to Crompton's, the

prosaically named restaurant. Once we were seated, Zoe excused herself. I looked around at the '80s décor—geometric wallpaper friezes and shiny curtains. When she returned, we took up our menus and had a look at what was on offer. I had to wonder at the source of the recommendation when I saw that there was only one vegetarian choice, standard vegetable lasagna. It didn't really matter because they had a bit of seafood, and besides, I fancied cod and chips as it happened. Zoe chose a pepper steak that, when it arrived, didn't look all that great. But anyway, it was nice to catch up, clear the air, and have a good laugh. We had each other in stitches over our banana splits and coffee; it felt great to be hanging out again.

"Let's go," said Zoe abruptly, as we were on the last sips of our coffee. She went to the counter to pay the bill rather than receive it at the table. As we left, I wanted to ask if she was okay but decided to wait until we were outside, perhaps suggest a proper coffee at one of the cafés along the seafront. Before we reached the doors beyond the reception desk, Zoe stopped short and turned to face me.

"Look, I've booked a room in the hotel for the night," she said. "Spend it with me."

"You what?" I asked, shocked, before quickly realizing the situation. I was suddenly annoyed because I felt so gullible. "That's why you brought me to this restaurant! God, the food was rough. I knew there was something strange going on."

She spoke softly, as a porter passed us. "You're right, and yeah, the restaurant was the unconvincing part of the plan, but I wouldn't have done this if I'd thought for a second you'd say no. I took you by surprise a couple of weeks back, but I know you've been thinking about it since. I don't think sex has to complicate a friendship. We're close, you and me. Let's see how far that goes."

"Zoe, I don't know." She was right, of course, I had given it thought.

"Well, I do. I know you and I know what excites you. That thing that you want, I've got it upstairs."

She wouldn't, surely. But then—she had to mean that. We'd had a specific conversation about it recently. I stood there, feeling like I was on the verge of something new. I could take this opportunity, or I could reject it and maybe always regret it.

"Show me what you've got, then," I said, eyeing her steadily to feign confidence.

Her face broke into a grin, and she hit the button to call the elevator. I expected her to leap on me the moment the mirrored doors closed, but she maintained a composed distance, heightening the anticipation.

The doors opened on the fourth floor. I followed her down the corridor and waited as she turned the key in the lock. The room was clean and simple, and had an enormous bed with crisp white linen. Zoe dimmed the lights as we entered. I peered through the curtains at the streetlights twinkling along the boulevard below. By day, the view of Oriental Bay must be spectacular.

Zoe rummaged in the fridge and pulled out cans of ginger ale, my favorite. On the table was a bucket of ice, which she must have arranged earlier. She handed me a drink and picked up the TV remote while she sipped her soda.

"Well," she said as she flicked through the channels, "I didn't invite you up here to watch the soaps." She found the channel she was looking for, flung the remote on the table, and turned to face me. Behind her, the TV emitted a blue light and soft moaning sounds. She put her drink down and approached me, reaching her arms out to wrap around my waist. We began to kiss, hesitantly at first, and then passionately. I felt her grip my arse and pull me closer, right in to her pelvis. She moved her lips to my ear and murmured, "I think you're so fucking horny. You try to contain it, don't you, but you're a dirty little minx."

I felt myself go limp at those words. She knew I liked dirty talk! This was nothing like sex for the first time because Zoe knew what pressed my buttons, and she wasn't going to play fair. *All right then,* I thought.

"Yes I am, as a matter of fact," I murmured back as I slid my hands up her top and cupped her breasts in my hands. On one level it felt weird—I had my friend's breasts in my hands. On another, it was erotic, plain and simple. I lifted her T-shirt and began to lick at her nipples.

"Oh," she began, and threw her head back. I flicked my tongue over and over her hard nipples and slowly drew them into my mouth. She had lovely breasts, firm and very full, and I buried my face in them. "Oh," she breathed again, "oh, but I have something for you." Soft sounds of moaning came from the television in bursts.

She maneuvered me over to the bed, pushed me onto it, and then stripped me down to my underwear. Blue light played across her as she pulled off her T-shirt and now-tangled bra and went over to her backpack. "Do you know what I've got for you?" she said, as more of a statement than a question.

I lay propped up on my elbows and grinned. "I couldn't possibly imagine." But I was imagining all right.

She retrieved a bottle of lube, and then watched my face as she reached into the bag again and pulled out a thick purple dildo. I drew in a breath.

"You said you wanted to try it, so I thought I'd make the arrangements. Like any friend would."

"Aah, well, that's some friend," I said, grinning. I was stunned by Zoe. God, she was bold! "Bring it here so I can see it," I said, sitting up on the bed. I couldn't believe it—we'd talked about strap-ons so recently, and I'd confessed that I was desperate to try it out.

"In a minute." She placed the dildo on the table and began to unzip her leather trousers, revealing a harness already fitted underneath. And no underwear.

She laughed to herself. "When I picked you up from your place, you hugged me. I was sure you'd feel the outline of the harness, and my plan would have been blown!"

"I didn't notice a..." I trailed off, transfixed, as I watched Zoe pull off her leather trousers and insert the dildo into the harness, finally jerking the straps tight to hold it in place. The thick cock extended from her crotch at a right angle, and I felt myself overcome with excitement and curiosity. Any apprehension had evaporated and was squarely replaced by a desire to explore.

"So, you wanted to take a look at it?" She approached the bed, the leather straps tight across her smooth brown hips.

She stood in front of me with her legs apart and her hands on her hips. Sitting on the edge of the bed, I slid my legs between hers and grabbed her bare arse to pull her closer. I began to touch the dildo, feeling its texture and girth. Her breath came a little faster, and I noticed moisture at the tops of her thighs as she watched me explore the strap-on.

Stroking its length, I looked up at her. "But how did you know what size to get?" I purred.

"You once told me how many fingers you like when you're really wet. So that's the girth I chose." I was impressed by her attention to detail. She continued, "It all started when we first discussed it. You said you wanted to try strap-on sex. I could tell you got kind of horny when you talked about it, so I decided to take the risk. As for aesthetics, you said you'd never have something that looked like a real dick, and I know purple is your favorite color. So you see, I knew exactly what you wanted because you told me. If I wanted to take it further, I'd say that you asked me."

"You're cocky, aren't you?"

"Nope, I just know what I see. I can make a good guess and say that right now you're sopping wet. Aren't you?"

I was beginning to feel too challenged, too exposed. I decided it was time to turn the focus to her. Ignoring her questions, I slid my hand up between her legs and teased the leather straps apart. Her wet and swollen pussy enveloped my fingers immediately. "Snap," I said as she quivered. "You should also know that I like butch bottoms, so you're not going to get very far if you insist on trying to top me. How about we call a truce, trust each other, and both give this a shot?"

"Okay," she exclaimed finally, her eyes rolling back as I continued to play at her pussy and make the straps slide repeatedly over her clit. "So long as I get the pleasure first—of giving it to you, that is."

Zoe pulled me down onto the floor. Filled with anticipation, I parted my legs so that she could get between them, but rather than fuck me she buried her face in my cunt, lapping at me with considerable skill, with that crimp-edged tongue of hers. For a moment, I languished in the heavenly pleasure of it before I writhed away. "No, I don't want to come this way!" I said. By now, I was completely sold on the idea of that purple dildo and didn't want to wait a moment more.

"All right, you asked for it," she said. "Are you sure you're ready?"

I gazed up at her. "Fuck me," I said, feeling like a pervert, like a libertine. This was all so new, and things were coming out of my mouth that my politics wouldn't have previously allowed. "I want you to fuck me, Zoe."

Zoe didn't need to be told again. She glided up my body until we were face-to-face. We began to kiss again, deeply, as she slipped the head of the dildo back and forth over my clit, wetting it with my juice. "No need for lube, then," she whispered. I began to writhe beneath her with utter urgency. She didn't make me wait. Watching my face, she guided the dildo in slowly until we were pelvis to pelvis. It was a wondrous feeling, but it was also conceptually erotic. Having a woman inside me in this way was so much more than I'd imagined.

"You cool?" she asked, checking in.

"Yeah, I'm cool!" I panted, as I arched my back again to meet her pelvis. Zoe began to strengthen her body somehow, tensing muscles in her thighs and arse. She locked her position using her knees and began to thrust into me with long, sure strokes. There was a sinuous quality to the way her body moved, controlled and rhythmical as she plunged in and out of me. My hips rose to meet her thrusts, and I clawed my nails into the hotel carpet to prevent myself from being fucked across the floor. Moans fell out of my mouth with the panting that came faster and faster now.

Beads of sweat had formed on Zoe's brow, and her own breath was labored. I could see that she was getting off on this just as much as I was. She began to grunt with each thrust, and her eyes rolled back so that only the bottom half of her irises were visible below her eyelids. Her face kind of screwed up then, and she really gave it to me. It was this force that finally pushed me over the edge. I came while she continued to fuck me, my hips arching again and again. Sighs rose up from my belly and burst out of my mouth as I spasmed beneath her. She stayed on top of me until my orgasm finally slowed to a shudder.

"Come here," I said, pulling her face toward mine and kissing her soft lips.

"So, I guess I was right, then," drawled Zoe. "I did have what you wanted upstairs!"

"Actually," I said, tapping her temple, "I'm totally into what you have upstairs—that's where the real sexiness comes from." I began to realize that Zoe had shown me a part of herself that I'd never seen before, one that no talk about sex could have revealed. And what I said, I meant. She was incredibly sexy. "But if you mean the strap-on," I answered, "then yes, it's fucking great!"

Now that my orgasm had passed, Zoe withdrew from me slowly and got up. I climbed into the bed, and she handed my drink to me. The now surely exhausted actors continued to fuck on screen, though the lighting had changed to a rosy glow.

Zoe topped up both of our drinks, and then gulped hers down in one go. "Thirsty work!" she said, grinning. As she began to take off the strap-on, I noticed how the still-wet dildo shone in the light. I liked the brazen, in-your-face element of this new toy—there was no mistaking what it was for. Zoe laid it on the table and climbed in beside me, lying on her back and stretching out. I propped myself up on one elbow and looked at her. She really was very beautiful. I'd never noticed what an attractive woman she was. Yet here I was, struck. I began to trace my fingers over her chest ever so lightly, careful not to touch her breasts at first. She sighed a little, and then smiled at me. I began to dance about her nipples with my fingertips, caressing them into hard candies.

"Ahh," moaned Zoe. Her hand snaked down her body. She buried her fingers in her pussy and began to rub herself while I played with her nipples and brought my lips to hers. She opened her mouth and our tongues met, slipping and sliding. I moved my face to her ear and sucked at her earlobe. "Mmmn, yeah," mumbled Zoe. I gently grazed her earlobe with my teeth before releasing it and whispering in her ear, "I believe it's my turn now...or your turn, depending on how you look at it."

Zoe opened her eyes slowly and looked at me, while continuing to lazily stroke her pussy. "Cock up then," she said, "and let's see what you can do. I have a feeling it'll be your forte." Without hesitation, I reached for the strap-on, still wet with juice.

SABRA

Lux Zakari

I bet I could change your mind, Mrs. B," Sabra said with a smile as we stood next to each other on the pavement. She continued to hold open the limo door for me, the gold streetlight making her dark skin seem luminescent. The night's crisp air turned her breath into clouds.

I stopped scrambling in my purse for her tip and froze, startled. "Change my mind about what?" I had no idea what she was talking about, but my skin prickled anyway.

"Everything." She purred the words as she urged me back into the limo.

For the past few hours she'd been driving me to my meetings, just as she had the last time I'd been in the city. She'd shown up at my door with a cocked hip and a crooked, knowing smile, but had remained professional all evening. Despite that, every glance she shot me in the rearview made my heart pound; no one had ever looked at me with such intensity, such *want*. I was sure she'd gotten a sneaking suspicion of the sudden, inexplicit dampness between my legs by the way I'd nervously cleared my throat and looked down at my hands, clenched in my lap.

Now we were parked across from my hotel on a quiet street, and although her duties were technically considered to be over, she clearly had other things in mind.

Sabra closed the limo door behind her and sat down next to me on the leather seat, still wearing that mysterious smile. She pulled off her black chauffeur's cap, shaking her braids free. Her fingers went to the giant gold buttons on the front of her uniform and she undid them slowly, watching my face for any reaction. When she opened her top, her naked breasts sprung free, presenting her already stiff nipples.

I sucked in a gulp of air and tried to will my body to stop shaking. This all was certainly different from the last time she'd driven me to my meetings, which had just been a few months ago, when I was still married and spent the majority of the time in her limo arguing with my ex-husband on my cell phone. She'd remained silent, but I'd seen her knowing smirks in the rearview mirror. At any rate, now it looked like she wanted to take me on a different kind of ride.

She pushed me so my back was pressed flush against the leather seat and straddled my body. She didn't even bother to kiss me as her lips seared the delicate skin of my throat and her hands kneaded my breasts over my wool peacoat. The sensations she was creating in me clouded my head, but I still managed to grab her thin wrists and choke out, "What are you doing?"

"Anything you want," she said, and added with a grin, "that I want, too." She finally kissed me, and in that moment I was reminded of smoky bonfires, wild blooming orchids, and pristine white beaches at night. I moaned as her fingers slipped inside my coat to unbutton my silk shirt.

"I know you need this," she continued. "I can tell." She

pushed my bra upward on my chest, exposing my small breasts, and coaxed my tiny nipples to life. They hardened beneath her touch, and her mouth left mine to travel down to my left breast. Her teeth scraped at the sensitive skin there, and I whimpered, not knowing whether to beg her for more or to beg her to stop.

I'd never been with a woman before, aside from kissing my high school best friend once during a game of spin the bottle. But that had been an attempt to show how sexually liberated we were at the ripe age of fifteen, as well as to seduce a roomful of teenage boys who couldn't believe their good luck.

This—with Sabra—was significantly different. To Sabra, it seemed like men didn't exist. At least, that was the impression I'd gotten the last time I saw her. My meeting had ended early, and I'd headed back to the limo only to find her sandwiching a coat-check girl between her body and the vehicle, oblivious to the stunned and intrigued looks that the men passing by were shooting them. It was clear that Sabra didn't want men, she didn't need them, and she certainly didn't feel compelled to seduce them. There was something exciting and free about that. Still, that meant her want for me was genuine, and that frightened me.

"I don't know about this," I admitted. Her hand had drifted down to the top button of my pants.

"Why is that?" She smiled, flashing me a row of charming, semicrooked white teeth. She wasn't taking me seriously—I could tell by the way she undid that top button and went for the second one.

"Because." My cheeks turned pink with shyness. "Look, I'm not—"

"You don't have to be anything you don't want to be," she assured me as she undid the last button and pulled my pants down over my hips and off my legs, revealing my lace thong panties with the butterfly appliqué. "But one thing you are is horny. And no matter what you *are* or *aren't*, you want me. I know that much."

How did she know? Did it even matter? She was right; more than right, in fact. I was feeling more excited than I ever had toward my ex-husband, a lawyer who had a mind for business and not a clue about a woman's needs. I had a feeling that Sabra didn't have his same problems.

"Have you ever eaten pussy before, Mrs. B?" she whispered, her voice thick with amusement and sensuality as she slid off my lap and knelt on the floor of the limo. She lowered her head to dip her tongue inside my belly button.

I swallowed hard. "It's just Kent now. Rachel Kent. I'm not married anymore."

"Good to know," she said, her voice still smiling. Her head moved lower, and her teeth scraped at my inner thighs. A moan of anticipation escaped my lips and intensified as her tongue slid inside the crotch of my panties. "These are very sexy panties, by the way. Too bad we have to get rid of them."

She dragged the thong off my legs, leaving me wearing only my coat, my unbuttoned shirt, and my bra up around my neck. I was still half-clothed, yet feeling more naked than I ever had in my life. My mouth opened to protest, but no sound came out.

Sabra opened my legs, and the cool air of the car against my hot cunt made my legs shake. Then she bowed her head again and swept her tongue over my pussy. The feeling was so different from when Edward used to go down on me. He had been hesitant and insecure with his tongue—even a little disgusted. Sabra, however, lapped at me with the tongue of a tiger and sucked on my clit as if it were hard candy. I gripped the seat and felt the leather grow wet under my sweating hands as I writhed under her spell.

But she pulled away, her face glistening with my juices. "It's time you gave it a try, Ms. K." Her dark eyes laughed at me, but I didn't care; I wanted her so badly.

"I don't know how—"

"Follow my lead." She grabbed my hands and pulled me onto the spacious floor of the limo with her. I tugged off the rest of my clothes and watched as she quickly unbuttoned her pants and kicked them off. Realizing that she'd been naked underneath her uniform all night sent a rush of heat straight to my cunt, but the sight of her naked, shaved mound made my mouth go dry with both fear and want.

"I'll show you what to do," she said, clearly recognizing the panic in my eyes. She grinned and reached for me. "Just bring that fine ass of yours over here first."

She positioned me over her, my thighs hugging her head and her pussy in my face, intoxicating me with its heady scent. I felt her mouth on my clit, so I took a deep breath for courage and mimicked her, flicking my tongue over the sensitive tip of her solid bud. Her moans and trembling legs urged me on and gave me a confidence I had never felt before. I copied her motions and played out what I knew *I* liked. I made a *V* with my fingers to spread her outer lips apart, exposing her pulsating clit. I caressed her pussy with my tongue, growing more brave and adventurous with her every whimper. She moaned into my cunt, vibrating my clit and sending tremors all through my body.

Sabra slid a finger into my tight cunt, and I let out a groan, my hands digging into her hips. I followed suit by pushing a finger inside her, and sucked on her throbbing clit as her mouth persisted in fucking me out of my mind. She added another finger in my dripping cunt, causing me to shudder and do the same to her. I could feel myself approaching my climax, but I didn't want to let up on Sabra now. I swirled my tongue over her clit until I felt her cunt close around my thrusting fingers and her hips buck upward toward my face. Her thighs clamped around my ears, muffling the sound of her screams in the limo.

Seconds later, electricity zipped through my bloodstream and headed straight for my clit. My body trembled and shook, and I rocked up and down as I came, burying her face in my pussy. I waited until I'd stopped shaking before I collapsed onto the floor next to her, whimpering while my cunt continued to twitch with aftershocks.

We lay there in silence, slick with sweat, our bodies used, exhausted, and satisfied. I took a few deep breaths as I waited for my heart rate to return to normal. I wondered how to proceed from here, not just tonight but for the rest of my life.

"I hate to say this, but I need to get this baby back." Despite her casual tone, Sabra's eyes were apologetic and sincere; she wasn't just trying to get rid of me.

"Of course." I tried to sound as casual as she did. We got dressed fairly quickly, and she opened the door for me to step out on my wobbly legs.

"I'll walk you up," she said, her eyes twinkling as she offered me her arm.

"You don't have to."

"I insist."

"All right," I said, suddenly feeling shy again. I held on to her elbow as we walked up the steps to the front door. I admired the way she moved, so unashamed and with no regrets. Right then, I wanted her more than ever. I wanted to be her.

We reached the front door, and I snapped open my purse, looking for my wallet. Sabra held up her hand. "No need. It was my pleasure."

"Oh. All right." A deep crimson flush spread over my cheeks as I realized the implications of my actions. The tip had been intended for the driving portion of the evening, and she smiled, assuring me that she understood.

"I hope you found everything to your liking, and that you'll call on Valvani Limousine Service in the future," she said, spicing up the requisite business script with her enigmatic grin.

"I will," I promised, and watched her walk down the path back to her limo. As she yanked open the driver's side door, I blurted out, "Thanks for the ride."

Sabra gave me a wink and tipped her cap at me. "You know it, Ms. K." She slid behind the wheel and pulled away from the curb, and I stood on the top step and stared long after the limo had glided down the street and out of sight, well aware that she'd not only changed my mind, but opened it as well.

PERIOD PANTIES

Anna Watson

Dale was a good-looking butch, in a me-big-macho-guy kind of way. Not a whiff of lesbian about her, just 100 percent prime male meat with a bossy attitude and a rigid view of exactly who wears the pants—which is fine if you like that kind of thing, and god help me, I do. There's something about that smug, god's-gift-to-femmes 'tude that speaks to me where it counts.

Dale and I met in someone's loft, at a party for someone's birthday or an art show or I don't remember what. She was loitering by the keg, cruising heavily, obviously looking to get laid. Getting laid was a high priority for me, too, and watching her preen in her muscle tee, flexing those biceps for anyone who cared to admire them, I started to salivate. When she not-so-subtly adjusted her package, I skipped over there, lickety-split, all ready to let her make the first move.

"Don't I know you from somewhere?" she said, predictably.

I played along, smiling into her eyes—she was just my height, and yum, do I love a built little butch—and saying shyly,

"No, I don't think so, but getting to know you might be nice."

It was simple from there on, and we ended up fucking in the bathroom after I hastily scrawled OUT OF ORDER in lipstick on the door. The sex was fantastic, made all the more so by her overconfident, well-rehearsed moves, from the little words she whispered in my ear as I straddled her, to the ardent way she promised she would call when we said good-bye. Surprise, surprise, she did call—must have been a slow week—and we tumbled into a low-key dating/fucking kind of thing. I loved her macho attitude, the casually disrespectful way she spoke about femmes, how she always made sure to check herself out every time we passed a mirror or a store window. I even loved that she wore a little too much cologne. What can I say? That kind of just-this-side-of-sleazeball boi makes my pussy smile. She could get it up and keep it up, too, which was a bonus, since a lot of these butches in my experience talk a whole lot more than they can fuck. So we were having fun together, but I knew it wouldn't last. I figured Dale was good for a maximum of three months before she got bored and moved on, so I made the most of her while I had her, getting her to fuck me in elevators, taxis, and back alleys. Public sex has always been one of my little kinks, and Dale was just as hot for it as I was.

About the tenth time she called for a date, I could hear in her voice that it was almost over. She'd probably met someone else, or was imagining that I was starting to get clingy and demanding and thinking about commitment—as if! I could see the way the wind was blowing, so I decided I might as well get something out of our last time together. I didn't think I was up for much, because I had my period and even Motrin hadn't taken care of the killer cramps. But a massage would be just the ticket, so I invited her over. Butches like Dale are always ready to give a girl a massage. It's a pride thing, and I think it's in the butch manual, under the section "Letting Her Down Easy."

Sure enough, when I answered the door, Dale had that distant, slightly put-upon expression that precedes The End. She looked even more pained when she saw that I was wearing my comfy sweats and an old T-shirt with no bra; up until now, I'd dressed up real pretty for her, every time. Tonight, though, what was the point? I was sure she was going to massage and run, and really, that was fine by me. They're no fun anymore once they think you're tooling for a diamond.

"I'm so glad you came over," I said, pouting a little. "I have such bad cramps!"

"I bet a massage would feel good," she said automatically. It was like she couldn't help herself. I pouted some more, grabbed her hand, and led her into the bedroom.

"I just have to run to the bathroom," I told her. "The massage oil is right there next to the bed."

It took me a little while in the bathroom because I'd had serious leakage and had to do some damage control. And I guess I was kind of quiet walking down the hall, because when I got back to the bedroom, I caught Dale going through my panty drawer. Well, this was not entirely a surprise—I immediately realized that of course she would be looking for a little token of her latest conquest—but what I hadn't expected was what she was holding. It wasn't my purple leather thong. It wasn't my crotchless black and reds. It was not my Hello Kittys or my cream-colored boy shorts. It was an old, nasty, ugly, ripped-up, stained-as-hell specimen that she must have dug up from some prehistoric part of my drawer. She had it wrapped around her nose and mouth, and her eyes were closed. She was swaying slightly.

This was not in the script. I was supposed to come back, find she'd prepared my bed for the Last Massage, lie down, get expertly pummeled, and then never see her again. I blinked, and must have made a sound, because she opened her eyes and froze. We looked at each other. I felt a flush rising in my cheeks. There was an expression in her eyes I'd never seen there before. She was ashamed.

"Dale," I said slowly, my voice calm and firm. "What do you think you're doing?"

Slowly, she lowered the panties, looking from them to me, her eyes big with—could it be a tinge of panic? She began to stammer something, but I stopped her with an imperious shake of my head. Who was in charge now?

"No, Dale, I don't want to hear your excuses. I see that you've rudely and without permission been in my lingerie drawer. I see what you're holding in your hand. And I think you know what a very, very bad boi you've been." I don't know what came over me. I've never thought of myself as a top, or anything like that—just the opposite, really—but now the powerful words came flowing out of my mouth. I stood tall and proud and so masterful, you would have thought I was wearing a rubber catsuit, thigh-high spiked boots, and carrying a big whip instead of being in what basically amounted to my pj's. And the rush I was riding rivaled the one I got when I finally figured out I was a butch-loving femme and not a regular lesbian. Sex before that had been good, and then it got great. Was it about to get even better? Dale huddled there with a seriously sexy helpless, guilty expression on her face, obviously as surprised as I was at the way things were going. I wanted to see more of that expression.

In the part of my mind that was still observing and trying to make sense of things, I wondered for a moment if Dale was going to go for it. But then she took the panties down from her face, folded them reverently, and offered them to me on the palms of both hands.

"I'm sorry," she said in a small voice. "I've been inexcusably rude."

"I will consider accepting your apology. Now, strip."

Again, I wondered if she would just leave—she never took her clothes off to fuck, not even when we were safely inside—but she was looking at me hungrily, and the energy between us was practically bouncing off the walls. She glanced around for somewhere to put the panties since I hadn't taken them from her, and finally replaced them gently in the drawer. She undid her belt, hands trembling, and let her jeans drop. She stood hunched over in her boxers for a moment and then kicked them off, leaving her dick exposed and swaying sweetly at attention. She pulled off her shirt and binder and stood naked in front of me, her eyes searching mine, her face bright red, her breath ragged.

I liked what I saw, this cocky butch exposed to me, her medium-sized breasts with the marks from her binder now swelling out from her body, the lush pubes that curled around the base of her dick. It made me feel mean.

"On your knees!"

She hit the floor. Seeing her at my feet gave me such a rush that I had trouble finding words, so I just slapped her, hard, one cheek, then the other. Her breathing speeded up, and she put a hand on her dick.

"Stop that!" I growled. "You are not to touch yourself. You do not deserve to touch yourself. You're disgusting." Moaning a little, she removed the hand and lowered her eyes.

I reached over and got my stained panties out of the drawer. They really were awful, ones I wore on my heaviest days, when I just knew I'd end up leaking. The persistent stains, left there period after period no matter how hot the water or how much bleach I used, were like a Rorschach test. I held the panties up in front of her face.

"What were you doing with these?" I hissed.

She swallowed hard, and looked pleadingly into my face. "I...I like them. I just like them."

"Address me properly!" I was practically shrieking, I felt so good. I dropped the panties onto the rug and slapped her again using both hands, a volley of sharp, stinging blows anywhere I could reach on her body.

"Yes, Ma'am! Sorry, Ma'am! How shall I address you?" I liked the way she was taking my slaps, not trying to get away, just flinching as she allowed them to land. I smacked her right across the tits.

"Ms. Weinhart will do, or Ma'am. Continue." I slapped her on the belly this time. I thought I could come from slapping her.

"Please, Ma'am! Ms. Weinhart! I have a collection. Of...of panties. Like these!" She nodded at the panties on the floor, and I could see the longing in her eyes. I nudged them with my toe, and I swear she gasped. I ground them into the carpet, laughing.

"A collection?" She lowered her eyes, her cheeks on fire from embarrassment and slaps. "You really are foul! What do you do with your gross little collection? Answer me, pig!"

"I, well, I guess I kind of jack off into them."

I closed my eyes for a moment to savor that image. I could hear her trying to catch her breath below me; I knew she was desperate to pick up the panties but didn't quite dare. I murmured, "You may."

When I opened my eyes, she was kneeling again, holding the panties up over her head. She had smoothed them out and folded them very nicely.

"You have a collection." I didn't know I could sound that sarcastic, that nasty. "Well, that is no more than I expected from a feeble slut-boi like you. Aren't you just a little cunty slut?"

She looked mortified, but she was nodding eagerly.

"Yes."

"Yes, what?" I grabbed the panties out of her hands and shoved them in my pocket.

"Yes, Ma'am!"

I surveyed her, walking around her kneeling figure. Her tight little asscheeks were clenched together, her body quivering. I put my foot between her shoulder blades and shoved her forward onto her belly, paying no attention as she squirmed on the floor trying to find a comfortable position that didn't squash her tits and her hard cock. I pulled my hand back for more slaps, but then had an inspiration. My brush was on my vanity table. It's a nice brush, with a broad, flat wooden back and wooden bristles. Good for keeping my curly hair tangle free. I made her crawl over and bring it to me in her teeth, like a good dog. Then she raised her cute little butt up for me, cradling her head in her arms. God, it felt good when I brought my brush down on her ass! I thought about her swaggering over here tonight, intending to give me my walking papers now that the shine had begun to wear off, with no interest in getting to know me as a person, no interest, really, in me at all. I was just one in a string of all-alike, paper doll femmes. How dare she dismiss me so casually? I was furious, and I brought the brush down over and over.

"Please, Ma'am, no more, no more!" I forced myself to stop pounding her, although I could have gone on for hours. The firm flesh of her asscheeks was splotchy and red, and when I touched it, squeezing it to make her gasp, it was wonderfully warm.

"Pussy butch," I sneered. "My other bois can take one hundred times more!" Needless to say, I didn't have any other bois, but it sounded good, and I could tell it made her feel shitty. I couldn't stop grinning to myself. "Roll over," I said, keeping my voice hard and mean. "Sit up." She did, her eyes shining with tears and lust as she glanced up at me.

"I'm sorry, Ma'am," she said, "I'll try to do better."

"Yes, you will." I took off my shirt and fondled myself. I could see her sneaking peeks; I knew how much she liked my teacup-sized breasts, my long nipples. I tugged at one of them, and she went to put a hand on her cock again, but thought better of it. I liked the way her hand was shaking.

"Please, Ma'am, may I...?"

"No, whatever it is, absolutely not. And shut up. Don't talk unless I ask you a direct question."

I continued playing with my breasts for a while, torturing her, until the pressure building up behind my clit was too much.

"Get up and put these on!" I took the panties out of my pocket and threw them at her, laughing as she missed the catch. She struggled to her feet, all wobbly, and managed to slide into them. They were way too small and looked ridiculous, with their little pink and blue flowers, the stained crotch barely able to contain her hard-on. I burst into laughter.

"Look at the period whore! What a sight you are, wearing my nasty, grimy panties! And you like it, don't you? Come on, admit it, you're loving getting to wear my filthy, blood-stained panties!"

She had lost all sense of restraint now. "Yes, Ms. Weinhart. I, yes, Ma'am. Thank you, Ma'am! I, I love wearing your panties, Ma'am! Thank you!"

The way she was looking at me, with such terrified respect, just about sent me over the edge. I shucked off my sweats and panties and sat down on my vanity table chair, leaning back comfortably and spreading my legs.

"On your knees. Crawl to me!"

She dropped with gratifying speed and obediently made her

way over to me, a ludicrous sight, tits dangling and my panties pinning her big dick close to her body.

"Get to work."

I thought she would dive right in like the eager doggy that she was, but she was really starting to show some imagination. Without being asked, she put her hands behind her back and leaned close but not touching. Her nostrils flared as she breathed in the rich, meaty smell of my pussy. Then she leaned over and put just the tip of her tongue on my thigh where the string of my tampon rested. She dabbed gently at the string, following it up to where it disappeared inside me, her gentle touch making me crazy. She began to swirl her tongue all up and down my slit, whimpering and breathing hard. It was all I could do not to grab her face and pull her to me, but I wanted this to last. I reached up to play with my nipples some more, and then placed a hand lightly on her head. Her moans as I handled her sent a jolt of pleasure through me. She was mine. I increased the pressure on her head, and she redoubled her efforts, burying her face in my cunt, tugging lightly on the tampon string with her teeth, lapping at my clit. At last, I couldn't stand it anymore, and clamping my thighs around her head, holding on to her and not caring one whit whether she could breathe or not, I rode her face until I came. It was a full-bodied thump of a come that left me sobbing for breath, my fingers moving absentmindedly over her head. She was such a good boi, keeping her hands behind her back and her face in my pussy until I'd gotten myself under control.

When I was breathing more or less normally and thought I could keep from looking too dreamy, I pushed her away from me. She lay on the floor, following me with her eyes as I brushed my hair and took a drink from the bottle of water I keep by my bed. I ignored the pleading look on her face. She clearly wanted to ask me if she could come, but was afraid to speak. I wouldn't mind watching her jerk off—yes, she could show me how she did it, that would be amusing—but I had other ideas for the time being. No, she could stay there, my little perverted period whore, naked except for my filthy period panties, groveling on the floor while I ordered her to lick my pussy again, suck my nipples, suck my toes, lick my asshole, until I'd had enough, and then maybe I would consider allowing her to touch her cock. Maybe. I'd think about it. Whatever I decided, though, one thing was for certain: this was going to be the best last date she'd ever had. And you'd better believe I was going to get my massage.

TASTING CHANTAL

D. L. King

A small cluster of smokers milled around outside the entrance to the club. Up and down the bar-lined street Neela noted the same phenomenon. The only difference was that absolutely everyone outside the Whip Handle wore black, whereas, while black seemed to be the predominant tone, other doorways also boasted a few girls in colorful spring dresses and boys in stone-washed denim and pastel shirts as well. The Whip Handle was like a sucking black hole after dark. It had rained earlier, making the sucking black hole shiny tonight.

Neela, of course, was no exception; after all, you don't go to a fetish club wearing a Hawaiian shirt and Bermuda shorts. She wore a black rubber pencil skirt, black seamed stockings, black stiletto pumps with chrome heels, and a black silk corset. If she'd draped a black veil over her head, she might have completely disappeared into total stealth mode. But she wasn't trying to disappear. To attract the kind of boys she was looking for, one had to be visible. Visible and scary.

"Neela!"

She turned, passed through the small crowd, and saw Kat. Smiling, she gave Kat a hug and kiss.

"I wouldn't have expected to see you here tonight, Neela," Kat said.

"Why not? Just because Sam left doesn't mean I'm dead. No, definitely not dead. I feel like playing, so I dressed to impress. Impressive, don't you think?"

"Yeah, but..."

"Later," Neela called over her shoulder as she swept through the door.

As usual, the place was dark and fairly crowded. She made her way to the bar and ordered a tonic with lime. Looking around, she noticed a few people she'd seen before but didn't really know. Oddly, almost all the people in the immediate vicinity were women. She saw a boy down at the other end of the bar, but he was obviously with the woman next to him.

Taking her drink, she made her way to one of the chambers off the main room, put down her toy bag, and made herself comfortable in one of the leather club chairs. A naked girl chained to the wall was being flogged by a large woman in black leather. Neela admired the woman's technique, and even in the dim light she could see red stripes on the girl's back and buttocks. After a few minutes she felt a slight pressure on the toe of her shoe. She raised her foot to bring the kneeling figure's head up, but the girl's eyes remained lowered.

"Yes?"

"Yes, Ma'am. This girl would like, um, this girl wonders if Ma'am would like, if Ma'am would be interested in...Um, this girl wishes to offer herself to Ma'am for use in any way she might see fit, ah, if she might wish to play with this girl, um—Ma'am.

The girl wore a short plaid schoolgirl skirt but was topless. She had very small breasts with petite pink nipples, almost boylike. The waistband of the skirt sat low on her hips, exposing her navel and the curve of her waist as well as the slightly rounded shape of her abdomen.

"I don't play with girls." Neela removed her toe from under the girl's chin.

Still kneeling, she looked up at Neela. "But then, this girl wonders why Ma'am would come tonight. Um, this girl means no disrespect."

"God, stop with the third person; I can't stand that stuff! What's your name?"

"This girl is called, I mean, my name is Chantal, Ma'am."

"Better. Okay Chantal, now what are you talking about? I come here all the time. Why wouldn't I want to come tonight?" Neela's eyes swept over the tasty mocha form of the girl still on her knees on the floor. She had honey-colored hair swept up into a messy bun on the top of her head, and striking olive-green eyes.

"Well, because it's girls' night. Sorry, Ma'am. I mean, it's the second Saturday. The second Saturday is always girls' night. This girl just thought—I mean *I* just thought, I mean you were so beautiful—I mean you *are* so beautiful and I've seen you here on other nights and I had hoped because I was so excited to see you tonight I thought maybe you'd like... I just thought, wow, 'cause you came on the second Saturday and maybe you didn't want just boys and 'cause I always saw you and thought you were so hot and I...I'm sorry, I'll go."

Chantal's lips were full and pink; she licked them and they glistened. She wore no makeup. Neela wanted to drink the girl's skin, it was so clear. She reached out and stroked her cheek. "No, it's all right. Stay." Her hand moved down to Chantal's chin and her fingers found those lips, brushing and parting them as she rested a final finger on the girl's lower lip.

"How old are you, Chantal?"

"Twenty-three, Ma'am."

Twenty-three. The walls of Neela's cunt tingled. She was just a girl—and not only that, she *was* a girl—a girl with a rather boyish figure, but definitely a girl. Neela let her hand slide down the girl's neck onto her chest. Her fingers lightly traced over Chantal's nipple before she leaned in to lick it. Withdrawing slightly, she blew on the wet nipple and watched it crinkle and stiffen.

Chantal's eyes closed and she mumbled, "Thank you, Ma'am," more to herself than aloud.

Neela smiled and pinched the nipple between her fingernails. The girl's eyes flew open, and she said, quite plainly, "Thank you, Ma'am."

Well, maybe this once...It wasn't like she'd never thought of playing with girls, it was just that the opportunity had never arisen before, or she hadn't been looking for it. She'd been mourning the loss of Sam and hadn't played in a long time. She'd come out tonight for a release, and she was going to get one, goddamnit.

"Chantal, why do you want to play with me?"

"This girl..."

"Bup, bup, bup." Neela put her finger on the girl's lips. "What did I say?"

"Sorry, Ma'am. I forgot."

"So? Why me?"

"Well, this—*I've* watched you on other nights playing with your boy, and you're just so beautiful and kinda scary, sort of... And whenever I see you play, I always imagine that I'm your boy. I could be your boy, if you gave this girl, I mean *me* a chance...I could be..."

"You're very sweet. Who taught you to use that affected

third-person crap? Is there someone whose permission you need to play with me? I won't play with someone else's property without an invite."

"No, Ma'am, I don't belong to anyone, not anymore. I did, but now I don't. I just..." She looked like she was about to cry, but instead, she lowered her eyes and began again. "I used to belong to a mistress in Boston. She said that slaves didn't have any rights and weren't really people, so they should never use the *I* word when referring to themselves. She said they should never refer to themselves at all, unless their mistress made them, and then to show the proper respect by referring to themselves as property. She made sure we learned."

"How come you're not with her anymore?"

"I guess she got tired of me. She drove me to New York and left me at this club."

"What do you mean? When did she leave you here? How long ago?"

"Three months. I used to come here every night, waiting for her to come back, but then I saw you."

Neela watched the tears begin to roll down Chantal's face. Her heart went out to the girl. "Here now, you come sit up here with me," she said, patting her lap. She put her arm around the girl's shoulder and let the young slave snuggle against her neck. "That woman was an idiot. I really can't stand people like that. Now, no more of that referring to yourself in third person. Not with me. I don't like it." She patted the girl's thighs. "So you want to play with me, huh? I'm used to playing with boys, you know; I play rough."

"Yes, Ma'am, this girl likes it rough. I really like it rough."

"Mm, mm, mm, that's another slip. What are we going to do to make you remember that you're a person? I think a spanking's in order here," Neela said, smiling, her eyes twinkling.

A wide grin split Chantal's face, and she nodded her head. "Yes, Ma'am, I think you're absolutely right." She bent over and slid down until she was lying across Neela's lap and flipped her schoolgirl skirt up.

As Neela expected, Chantal wasn't wearing underwear. She had a perfect, round bottom, and Neela could just see her cleanly shaved pussy lips peeking out from between her legs. There were a few fading bruises on her cheeks and the backs of her thighs.

The first smack landed squarely in the middle of one cheek. She bounced a little, but otherwise made no sound. Neela landed another on the opposite cheek and then proceeded to cover the girl's bottom in light spanks until it bore a uniform pink blush and began to take on some heat. She moved her hand down between Chantal's legs to run her fingers over the girl's sex. So smooth, so different from a boy's sex. Chantal was obviously turned on, and feeling the girl's excitement excited Neela.

"You really are a very naughty little girl, aren't you? You're all wet down here." Neela grabbed the girl's cunt and squeezed until Chantal squeaked and the juices ran out between Neela's fingers.

Neela's spanks rained harder and harder on the girl's bottom while she ran her fingers through the girl's wet slit. She smelled the fragrance of the girl's arousal and noted that it was different from her own—similar, but different. The scent was a heady one, especially as she knew that she'd caused it. She sank her middle finger inside. It was a lovely, warm, moist feeling, but different than masturbating. The girl's muscles contracted against her finger, and Neela found herself warmed by the human connection. She slid her index finger inside to join her middle finger.

"Oh, thank you, Ma'am," Chantal moaned. She alternately pushed her bottom up to receive the smacks and thrust back against Neela's hand. Neela gently pressed and caressed the wall of the girl's hot, wet interior, over and over.

She felt the girl freeze against her legs, and then begin to squirm. Without changing the motion of her fingers, she stopped spanking. "What's the matter, little girl? Why so squirmy?" she said with a low chuckle.

"Please, Ma'am, may this girl come?"

SMACK! "What?"

"Sorry, sorry, sorry, but please, Ma'am, I have to come. Please."

"I don't think I should let you come. You obviously haven't learned your lesson." She slowly removed her fingers from the girl's cunt.

"Nooooo..."

"Oh, please. What, you thought this was about you? Poor little subby-girl—thinks she gets to come after ten minutes of playing. Right! No, I think you'd better come with me," Neela said, setting the girl on her feet and taking hold of her wrist. "Now, what shall I do with you? Ah, I know." Holding on to the girl, she strode purposefully toward the back of the club.

"Where are we going, Ma'am?" Chantal followed along behind with an ever-widening smile plastered to her face until Neela finally stopped in front of an unoccupied massage table.

"All right girl, hop up here and get comfortable. I don't think we need this skirt right now, do we?" Neela took the skirt, folded it, and put it on a nearby bench. She attached the girl's ankles to cuffs at the sides of the table, spreading her legs as wide as the table would allow.

Chantal sat up to watch as her legs were fastened to the table. When Neela finished, she turned around and put her palm against the girl's chest. Once Chantal was flat against the table again, Neela fastened her wrists to cuffs at the top of the table.

"I'm going to examine you. I've examined lots of boys, but never a girl. With you fastened and spread like this, I can take my time and get a good look at you." She could see that her words were having their effect on the girl as Chantal began to squirm against her restraints a bit and her breathing quickened.

"Look at these pretty little nipples." As she spoke, before she could even touch them, they both crinkled and stiffened. "Oh, that's so sweet, they're getting themselves ready for me." She lightly ran her fingers over both nipples at the same time.

Chantal shuddered.

Neela traced circles around and around the girl's areolas, making sure the nipples were as hard as they were going to get before pinching them between her thumbs and forefingers. She started out with a minimum of pressure, but gradually increased it until the girl moaned. She pulled them up, stretching Chantal's breasts and elongating her nipples.

"You have such sweet little breasts, almost like a boy's, but different." She pulled a little farther, finally letting the nipples slip from her grasp. Red and distended, they were irresistible to her, and she bent to run her tongue over the nearest one to the sounds of Chantal's soft moans.

Neela worried the nipple and its surrounding flesh with her tongue before backing away slightly and blowing on it. Placing her mouth back over it, she lightly bit the tiny nub of flesh with her teeth. Chantal rocked her body from side to side in response.

"Thank you, Ma'am."

"You taste sweet and fresh." Neela closed her mouth over the girl's breast and roughly grabbed the other in her hand, squeezing it while she sucked and licked the breast in her mouth. She watched the girl's body. The more pressure she put on Chantal's breasts, the higher the girl raised her hips off the table.

Neela liked the feel of the girl's breast in her mouth. Again, it was different from a boy's breast; soft, where a boy's breast was firm; smooth, where a boy's skin was slightly more textured. It was somehow—inviting.

Neela was brought back to reality by the sound of the girl's bottom smacking the table as she pumped her hips up and down. Neela heard the word "Please" several times before pulling her leather crop out of her bag and smacking the girl's wet breast three times in quick succession.

"Relax, I'm not finished with you yet."

Chantal whimpered and squirmed on the table. Neela softly ran her fingers over the girl's torso, moving to her sides to encircle her small waist. Chantal's curves, while understated, were still different from Neela's experience. She loved the feel of the girl's waist and the fact that it was so small.

She positioned her hands on Chantal's abdomen so that her fingers pointed toward her feet. She let the flat of her palms trace the natural *V* formed between the girl's legs. She squeezed the soft skin and tendons where Chantal's legs joined her body and saw a bit of moisture escape between her pussy lips. Chantal was probably drenched—Neela certainly was—and she wanted to dip her fingers inside to check, but instead she moved them back up to the top of the girl's shaved pubes. Pressing with her fingers, she pulled up, toward Chantal's waist, and her slit elongated, causing the lips to draw closer to each other.

"Oh, please, Ma'am," Chantal moaned.

Ignoring that, Neela slapped the top of the girl's pussy several times, until it took on a lovely rosy color and the moisture squished out from between the lips to splash under her hand. Not until then did she insinuate a finger between the labia. She explored the girl's clit, which had become more prominent, and listened to her heaving breaths. She gently pinched the nub of flesh and rolled it between her fingers before leaving it and moving on.

A whine escaped Chantal, which turned into a groan as a finger pushed itself inside her pussy. Neela couldn't believe how wet the girl was. She slid another finger inside, pumping in and out several times, listening to the squishing sound she made. Neela began slowly moving the girl's lubrication out of her pussy and down toward her anus as she pumped. Over and over, she brought moisture from the girl's sex to her anus. Neela found the scent of Chantal's arousal overpowering. As soon as the girl was lubricated enough, Neela pushed a finger inside her ass as she went down on her pussy. There was something about this girl. Neela had never been interested in the taste of pussy before, but she felt compelled to taste Chantal.

Chantal's hips thrust up off the table, pressing hard against Neela's mouth as she stabbed at the girl's opening with her tongue, drinking her juices. The taste was almost overpowering. Neela held her finger still in Chantal's ass while she pounded her pussy with her tongue. She moved her tongue up to press against the side of Chantal's clit and the girl immediately came, her limbs stiffening and vibrating uncontrollably as Neela continued the pressure against her clit.

Finally, Chantal's spasms subsided. Neela withdrew her mouth and slowly removed her finger from the girl's ass.

"I'm sorry, Ma'am. I'm sorry. I didn't mean it." Chantal said.

Neela kissed Chantal, painting the girl's face with her own juices. Exploring Chantal's mouth with her tongue, she realized that it was the first time she'd ever kissed a girl like this. The combined taste of the girl's mouth and her musk were sweet beyond measure. Neela's clit throbbed with need. "It's all right, girl. Would you like to come home with me tonight?"

"Really?"

"Yes, really. Would you?"

"Oh, yes, Ma'am, yes please."

Neela began unfastening the girl's restraints. "Fine, then we can talk about what you'll need to do to make up for coming without permission." She felt like she was swimming in her own juices. Thoughts of Chantal's mouth fastened to her pussy as she came over and over again made her want to rush to get the girl dressed and back to her apartment.

Once Chantal was standing, Neela embraced her and kissed her again, sliding her hands down over the schoolgirl skirt and under it, caressing the girl's bottom until she finally broke the kiss and slapped Chantal's ass. "Let's go."

OPENING NIGHT

Charlotte Dare

Her spiky black hair shone purple under the stage lights, and her movements were graceful as a dancer's. The night of auditions for Neil Simon's *Rumors,* Mari delivered the lines for Chris in a throaty drawl that would've made Kathleen Turner jealous. I couldn't peel my eyes off of her. The newest member of the Shoreline Players had a stage presence sure to steal every scene.

Throughout our six-week rehearsal schedule, I found myself shadowing Mari at every opportunity, chalking it up to professional admiration. In my early twenties, community theater was more than a creative outlet. It was an escape from myself, the chance to be someone else under the noble disguise of artistic expression. I may have been fooling myself, but looking back, Mari had me pegged from our first read-through.

"We have a great cast," she said as we left the theater. "You're going to make a wonderful Cassie."

"Thanks," I said, "but I can't picture myself as the perky

newlywed type. Of course, I don't tell my boyfriend that."

She nodded with mild amusement. "He must enjoy watching you perform."

"Eh," I began, tilting my hand from side to side. "But after sitting through *Macbeth* and *The Winter's Tale,* he said he'll be glad to see me in a play he can understand."

She smirked. "He's not a fan of high art?"

"Sadly, no," I said. "Unless it involves watching guys try to get a ball from one place to another, Jason's not interested. But he does do a good job faking it."

Mari chuckled as she twirled her car keys. "How does he feel about you spending so much time at rehearsals?"

"Not crazy about the idea. He doesn't come right out and say it, but he gives plenty of subtle clues." Before I knew it, Mari had walked me to my car under an orangey streetlight.

"Well, I wouldn't let anyone persuade you off the stage. From what I've seen, you're very talented." Her smile was forceful, and her eyes lingered on mine for an uncomfortably long time.

"Thanks." I felt my face flush. When she walked off to her car, I just stood there watching her. For the first time in years, I hadn't had to justify refusing to give up the stage to meet someone else's emotional needs.

I followed the taillights of Mari's Prius for about two miles until she took a right at a stop sign and they disappeared into the night. For a split second I actually thought of following to see where she lived. I should've known right then that something was happening, but the blinders were still securely in place.

By the end of the first week of rehearsals, I was getting more butterflies in my stomach waiting for Mari to walk in than I did thinking about opening night.

"How's it going, *Cassie*," she whispered as she plunked down in the chair I'd saved for her by throwing my leg across it.

"Hiya *Chris*." I smiled like a fool as I pretended to listen to the director drone on.

"Does anybody have any questions before we block the last scene in Act One?" he asked. "I know we're moving fast, but I want to start running the show as soon as possible."

"He does know we're not in the running for a Tony, doesn't he?" Mari drawled. I stifled a laugh.

Later, as Mari and I stood in the wings waiting for our respective cues, I had a heightened sense of her presence—the whisper of her deep breathing and the fruity smell of her hair gel as she leaned toward me and stretched—things I'd never noticed about anyone else I'd done a show with.

She crunched on a Granny Smith apple she'd fished out of her bag as she wobbled on her character shoes. "These damn things never fit right. I have to get a new pair." She tossed the core in the garbage and clutched at my shoulder, leaning most of her weight on me. "Don't mind me. I think I have a pebble in here."

I didn't mind at all. In fact, I relished the pressure from her hand as she balanced herself on one foot.

"There, that's better," she said. "Hey, are you going to the Cantina tonight for drinks?"

I hadn't planned to. Jason wanted me to meet him for coffee after rehearsal. "Are you?" I asked.

She raised an eyebrow at the absurdity of the question. "I teach kindergarten, so if I don't do happy hour with the faculty on Fridays, then you better believe I'm going out with the cast after rehearsal. Besides, the Cantina has the most extraordinary veggie nachos. We can take one car if you'd like to save some gas."

I thought about Jason's reaction and smiled in spite of myself. "Who doesn't want to save gas?"

"Since I have the hybrid, I'll drive," she said, and charged into her scene with fluid timing.

By around ten o'clock, six of us from the cast and crew had stuffed ourselves into a corner booth at the Cantina and were having a raucous time laughing at each other's scene flubs and slipups earlier in the evening. I was shoulder to shoulder with Mari, savoring every sensuous experience from the tangy taste of the appetizers and drink to the tickle of her firm arm brushing against mine to the clean scent of her patchouli oil. As an added bonus, Mari was a laugh-leaner—every time she laughed, she would lean into the person who'd amused her. The moment I realized this, I practically turned into a stand-up comedienne.

"You're a riot, Kim," she cooed after composing herself enough to take a sip of her raspberry margarita.

"It's true. You never realize how many words in the English language have *S* in them until you have a conversation with a person who lisps."

She giggled again, and just as I was in the midst of secretly congratulating myself, my cell phone sang "The Name of the Game" from the *Mamma Mia* soundtrack. I looked down and was horrified to see it was Jason calling. How could I have forgotten to call and tell him I wasn't going to meet him for coffee?

"I have to take this," I said with a dour expression, and then hurried into the hall near the bathrooms. "Hello?" I answered as if I had no idea what the call was about.

"Where the hell are you?" he bellowed. "I waited twenty minutes at the coffee house, and now I'm at an empty theater."

"I'm at the Cantina. I'm sorry. We were in such a rush I forgot to call you."

"Nice. So now you're blowing me off to hang out with the people you just spent all night with?" Suddenly, his clues weren't so subtle. "That's bullshit."

"Jason, I didn't mean to blow you off. Why don't you come

down here now and join us?" As soon as it came out, I hoped he wouldn't say yes.

He was still steaming. "I mean is this how it's going to be with this group?"

"Jason, you know part of the experience is hanging out and unwinding afterward. It's nothing against you. You said you understood about this kind of stuff."

"I do, but we had plans. I can't friggin' believe you forgot to call me."

He sounded so hurt, and as much as I wanted to get back to the table, I couldn't help feeling guilty. "Jason, I'm sorry."

"How much longer are you going to be down there?"

"An hour or so. Maybe less."

"Forget it. I'll just see you tomorrow night. We *are* still on for our anniversary dinner tomorrow night, aren't we?"

"Definitely. Good night." The abruptness in my good-bye did little to corroborate my contrition. I rushed back to the table and slid in next to Mari.

"You're not in trouble, are you?" she asked. The way she said it sounded more like a dare than an expression of concern.

"Of course not. I just reminded him this is what the cast does on Friday nights during the show. Isn't it?"

"I'd say so with this crew." She looked at me with eyes that brimmed with sensitivity. She understood something about me, although I had no idea what. I didn't know what to say at that moment, but I couldn't look away. "You are allowed to have a good time on your own, Kim." She patted my leg just above the knee and took another sip of her margarita.

As the weeks blazed on, I regularly caught myself thinking about Mari. At work, at home, spending time with Jason, it didn't matter—some random thought about her would sneak into my consciousness and sweep me away. The night of our anniversary, the last time Jason made love to me, I couldn't keep my mind from wandering. When he kissed me, I imagined it was Mari's lips trailing down my neck. When he penetrated me, it was with Mari's fingers. I actually orgasmed that night, but it wasn't Jason who'd brought me there. I left his place in the morning feeling dirty, trying to convince myself that those thoughts didn't mean anything. It had to be because I was spending so much time with Mari at rehearsal.

The Sunday before we opened, I called and asked her if she could run lines with me that night, not an unusual request save for the fact that I knew my lines cold. I was still steeped in vigorous denial, but once again, Mari was one step ahead of me.

After we'd run through the last scene, she plopped down on her sofa and raked a hand through her hair. "See? I told you there's nothing to worry about."

I collapsed in a cushy chair across from her. "Well, in live theater there's no such thing as too prepared."

"That's why I love performing with you. You have such respect for your craft." She grinned and crossed her legs on the coffee table, folding her arms behind her head. "So, you wanna tell me the real reason you're here? Does it have to do with Jason?"

Just when I'd thought I could relax. When, finally, my hands weren't shaking and I wasn't pulverizing breath mints to keep my mouth hydrated anymore. Now this. "What do you mean?" I stammered. "I'm nervous about the show."

"You're nervous about something, but I doubt it's the show. You haven't forgotten a line in rehearsal yet. Shit, you even know everyone else's."

I sighed and desperately tried to climb out of the hole I'd unwittingly dug. "All right," I lied. "It is about Jason." I conjured a pained facade.

"What's the matter?" Her tone was so warm and comforting; I just wanted to crawl into her lap.

"We're not getting along like we used to," I said.

"Is it you or him?"

"I don't know. We're fighting all the time, especially since I started the show."

"It's probably because he's feeling left out and missing you, that's all," she said. When I looked up from absently studying my cuticles, she was staring over at me with a seductive smile. "I can't really blame him."

I giggled but looked down again. The conversation was opening doors I wasn't prepared to move through. "But there's nothing wrong with him. He's a good guy. It must be me."

"Maybe it *is* you. You probably need some time to figure out what you want."

"What I want?"

She shifted her position to Indian-style on the sofa, her tanned toes peeking out from under her knees. "Maybe you don't want what it is you think you want."

"What do you mean?" I said, flustered. "Like maybe I want a guy with blond hair or a different job? I'm not sure what..."

"Maybe not a guy at all." She threw it out there as casually as if we were ordering Chinese food.

"I don't think so," I said with an anxious chuckle.

Mari smiled and shrugged. "It's not the end of the world if it's true."

"I know that. I'm cool with gay people. I have gay friends."

"Present company included, I hope." Another flirty smile.

Ripples of nerves shot through my stomach. "I should get going now. I have to get up for work in six hours."

She draped her hand around my shoulder as she walked me to the door. "Look, I wouldn't worry about anything, Kim.

I'm sure things will be fine with you and Jason after the show closes."

I stopped at the front door and gazed into her golden-flecked eyes. "Thanks."

"Any time." She rubbed the side of my shoulder. "Now relax. And think about everything I said. Just think about it."

As I walked down the stone steps, I wasn't sure which of Mari's parting words left me feeling so unraveled—that I might be gay or that things would indeed be fine with Jason again.

Opening night was electric. The entire cast's energy and timing were spot on, and for once, I delivered a nearly flawless performance. Mari hosted the opening night celebration after the show, cramming all of us into her quaint Cape on the beach. Although I enjoyed the company of everyone, my attention belonged solely to Mari. It was after one A.M. when the last guest left; last, that is, except me.

"Are you sure you're all right to drive home?" Mari asked as I lingered at the front door.

"I had one wine cooler two hours ago," I replied.

"I'll take that as a 'yes,' " she said. "That's too bad. Tomorrow's going to be a gorgeous day to relax out on the beach." She turned and glanced out her French doors at the moonlight bobbing on the choppy water.

Was she trying to get me to stay over? "It is kind of late, and I do live almost an hour away," I said.

She smiled knowingly. "I love it when the tide comes in this time of night. Would you like to look out at the water?"

"Sure."

We leaned over the porch railing together, resting on our elbows, listening to the waves roll onto her slip of private beach.

"Wow," I gushed. "It must be amazing to fall asleep to this sound every night."

"It makes everything more amazing." As she studied my face, her scent floated over me in the breeze.

She smelled delicious, and by now it was impossible to rationalize the way she was making me feel. She leaned in and gently kissed me. *I should protest, shouldn't I? Back away or something?* But I didn't want to. She cupped my cheek in her hand and kissed me again, slow, sensual kisses that were warm and wet and unlike anything I'd ever felt. I tingled all over as she wrapped her arms around my neck and pulled me to her, slowly exploring my mouth with her tongue.

"You're so beautiful, Kim," she breathed. She stroked my arms with her painted fingernails, giving me chills in the warm night air. "I'd love to make love to you," she whispered, and kissed my neck softly.

"I've never been with a woman before," I said as my knees buckled from the pleasure of her touch.

"I know, honey," she said, nibbling my earlobe.

Confused, nervous, and aroused beyond my wildest dreams, I wanted to hop over the railing and run away. "But I don't know what to do."

A low, sensual giggle vibrated in my ear. "You will when I'm through with you." She led me in through the French doors, leaving them wide open. When she switched off the living room lamp, the flickering votives on the mantel and the full moon peering in through the doors illuminated our faces.

We stopped at her oversized sofa and kissed some more. Her hands spread out widely over my body, caressing my arms and lower back under my shirt. I dared to slide my hands down to her ass and squeezed.

"Oh, Kim," she breathed.

I felt a surge between my legs like I'd never known. I was wet and throbbing and terrified. I'd never felt this with Jason or any other boyfriend. I didn't know what it all meant, but I knew I didn't want Mari to stop.

She pulled her own shirt off and then mine and lowered me onto her plush sofa. Her warm stomach felt so good against my skin as she licked my neck and exhaled in my ear. She unhooked my bra and dove onto my hard nipples, sucking one while rubbing the other. I wanted so badly to feel her fingers down there, to guide her hand onto me, but inhibition held me captive. So I lay there craving her as she slowly drove me insane with a marathon of erotic play.

When the last of our clothes finally came off, she kissed my stomach as she made her way down my body. The smell of the beach drifted in with the night breeze while Mari's tongue tickled my thighs. I clutched the sofa cushions at the warmth of her breath and smoothness of her fingertips fondling the backs of my legs. Before I knew it, her firm tongue was on my clit. She took her time whirling around, teasing me to the point where I practically begged her to make me come. Finally she penetrated me, thrusting in and out, riveting my body with intense pulses of pleasure.

Normally quiet during sex, I heard myself gasping and groaning, calling out Mari's name. I gripped the sofa cushions harder as my climax began rising, carrying me away to ecstasy. As I got louder, Mari grabbed my hips tightly and drilled her tongue into me until I came harder than I'd ever imagined doing. "Holy shit," I gasped as my legs shuddered.

She snuggled up to me while I caught my breath. "Did you like that?" she asked, and kissed my cheeks and nose.

"You were right. Everything's better by the shore."

After a few moments of nuzzling, Mari took my hand and placed it on her pussy. She was silky and wet, and she started slowly moving my fingers up and down, letting me take control gradually. She moaned in my ear and pumped away in time with the rhythm of my hand as she began climaxing. It was so hot watching her orgasm! She'd aroused me all over again.

It was somewhere around four A.M. by the time we were both satiated enough to fall asleep entwined in her Egyptian cotton sheets.

The next morning I sat on the warped wood of Mari's back porch watching the seagulls swoop down on the rocky shore at low tide.

"What are you doing up so early? It's only ten after seven," Mari said at the back door. When I didn't answer, she padded outside in her bare feet and sat down next to me. "Why are you crying?"

"I don't know," I said, wiping my cheek with the side of my hand.

She shaded her eyes from the bright morning sun. "Do you feel weird about last night?"

"No, last night was incredible. I think that's what's making me feel weird."

She gently rubbed my back. "Some people think coming out to the world takes guts." She shook her head with certainty. "Coming out to yourself takes more guts than anything."

"So am I a lesbian?" I asked, choking back my jumbled emotions.

Mari squeezed my shoulder. "I can't answer that for you, honey. But based on your responses last night, I'd say you're at least halfway there."

I laughed through a sob. "How do I find out for sure?"

"You have to be honest with yourself. It'll be easier to figure out if you can do that."

"I care about Jason, but I don't feel for him what I feel for you. I've never felt that way about any guy I've dated."

She grinned. "What do you feel for me?"

I sighed and just started babbling. "I don't know. I think about you all the time, and when I know I'm going to see you, I get all jittery. I hate saying good night, and at rehearsal, I hate it when you talk to other people. And when we're not at rehearsal, I try to think up excuses to call you. And sometimes when I look at you—I forget to breathe." I clammed up when I finally noticed the astonished look on Mari's face. "I'm in love with you, aren't I?"

"It would appear that way." She sighed and leaned forward, staring pensively out across the water.

"What's the matter?" I said, sensing her distance.

"I wasn't very responsible last night," she said, clasping her fingers together.

Her tone was disquieting. "What do you mean?"

"I knew you were attracted to me, but, god, I never thought you could be in love with me. I just figured it was an experience we'd both enjoy."

I cleared my throat bravely. "And you don't have those feelings for me."

"I didn't say that. The thing is I'm eleven years older than you. I've been out forever, and I'm comfortable with who I am and what I want."

I licked the last tear from my lip and felt my ears getting hot. "So then you used me?"

"No, of course I didn't. Frankly, I don't want to be used by you. I'd rather not be the test case that either sends you back the other way or serves as a springboard for your new life as a socially active lesbian. I really could fall for you, Kim, but I know the timing isn't right for us."

"How could you be so sure?"

She stood up and loomed over me, full of arrogance. "Because

I know how these things work; I've seen it before. Some older, supposedly wiser woman gets all worked up over an ingénue she leads to her sexual awakening, only to get dumped when the little dykling flies off to discover what treasures the exotic and enticing lesbian world has to offer."

I said nothing for a moment, challenging her with a cold, penetrating stare. "Fine, Mari. I get it. We had our one night of passion. You fucked me so good I could never go back to guys even if I wanted to. So now what? When the show closes, we just go our separate ways?"

"We'll have to play it by ear," she said.

I hugged my knees and fumed silently.

"Kim, we'd be making a huge mistake jumping into something."

"Maybe I should just stay with Jason," I said.

"And you'd be cheating two people with that decision," she said. She trudged back inside and stopped at the screen door. "Make that three."

We barely survived the three-week run of *Rumors*, thanks to my stubborn lovesick melodrama. When I wasn't shooting Mari evil glances across the wings, I was wrenching my arm from her grip backstage whenever she tried to draw me into a civilized conversation. But in the end, Mari was right. I needed time—time to part ways with Jason, to reconcile my own feelings and begin the coming-out process, all of which I needed to do on my own.

Mari's right about a lot of things and never one to gloat. Yet for some reason she's enjoyed reminding me of our *Rumors* days on every anniversary for the past five years.

GETTING IT

Jean Roberta

Two young women sat in the bar of an old, crumbling hotel. The beer-soaked wooden floor creaked under their feet, the bartender watched football on the television, a fat woman with brass-colored hair held hands with a bony man with a knife-scar on his cheek, and three men argued in low voices, their heavy rings flashing in the dim light. Outdoors, traffic swished past under a distant summer moon.

For the two young women, drinking in this bar was an adventure. Anything could happen here. "What are you afraid of?" asked Liane, brushing long black hair off her peach-toned face.

Peggy looked into Liane's deep brown eyes and then looked away. "Him and his friends. Getting killed."

"Understandable. But you had the guts to leave, girl, don't forget." Liane's expression was a cocktail of sympathy, interest, and desire. She sipped her margarita as though tasting fresh nectar from a woman she wanted. Liane's blue latex dress gleamed in the dim light, and the black-painted fingernails tapping out a rhythm on her glass were like shiny dancing beetles. "You must have had good times with him before he turned on you."

Peggy was pink-cheeked, red-haired, and voluptuous like a farmer's daughter in a dirty joke or a woman warrior in a video game. Her breasts filled her cotton blouse, confronting all comers. She looked as if she belonged in an open field. The flush on her face was as charming as the creamy pallor of her cleavage. "It was—yeah, incredible. We did things I hadn't done before. I—it was both of us. But then he'd pick fights with me over nothing and do things to get back at me. I couldn't stop him."

Liane licked her red lips. "Do you have bad dreams about him?"

Peggy leaned forward. "I can't get it out of my mind. Sometimes I don't want to fall asleep."

"Baby." Liane reached forward and held Peggy's nearest hand. "Do you trust me, girl?"

For an instant, Peggy looked trapped. Her eyes roamed from her rum-and-coke to the window on the street. She looked at Liane and laughed. "No. Hell no, Liane. You're not innocent. I mean, neither am I. I don't know who I could trust."

"I'm a woman like you, Peggy. So you know I'm different from a guy." Liane raised an eyebrow, and Peggy laughed. "You want a change, don't you? I could give you what you want. What did he do to you? What happens over and over in your dreams?"

Peggy stared and tried to pull her hand away, but Liane tightened her grip. "No," Peggy said.

"Think about it. What do you think would drive your nightmares away?"

Peggy shifted uncomfortably on a hard wooden chair. Liane knew her well enough to recognize the look on her face. Liane enjoyed breathing in her own signature perfume mixed with the musk from her armpits, and she knew it was the best smell available to Peggy in the stale air of the bar. "Want me, girl?"

"Oh, god." It was almost a whisper. Peggy seemed overwhelmed by unexpected desire. Liane gazed steadily at her, and then flicked a glance around the room.

One of the three men was staring at her and Peggy, sizing them up.

"You'll be a lot safer with me." It was a quiet but confident warning. "Let's go."

The two women stood up, and Liane wrapped an arm around Peggy's waist to guide her securely to the exit. Peggy's skin felt damp and cool, but Liane knew that the crotch of her pants must be damp and hot.

Coming out of the bar felt like coming out of the closet, leaving the funk of past pain behind and welcoming the fresh air of new experience. Liane and Peggy both loved the moment when they were going somewhere together and not just being watched by men. Each time they took this trip felt like the first.

Outdoors on the sidewalk, Peggy looked up and down the street. "We're not being followed," Liane told her. "Hold on to a little of that fear, though. It'll keep you focused." She wrapped a toned arm around Peggy's shoulders to lead her forward.

Liane's car was parked a block away. When Peggy slid into the passenger seat, Liane knew that she had signed on for the rest of the trip.

Liane pulled smoothly into traffic, feeling as if she were bringing a captive wild animal home to be nursed back to health. Peggy's energy filled the car.

Liane's cozy apartment on the tenth floor of a venerable building offered a sweeping view of the city. As she and her guest rose in the elevator, Liane grinned. "It's like living at the top of a very high tree, or a mountain cave. No one can get you up there except me."

Peggy pressed her sweaty breasts against Liane's. They stood entwined, soft lips clinging together, as they went up, up, up, exchanging breath and saliva.

Liane unlocked the door to her lair. The curtains at the window were open, letting in natural and artificial light from the moon and the nearest building. The shadowy apartment was as full of soft, fancy cushions as a sultan's harem. "Throw yourself down anywhere, Peggy," she invited. She pushed Peggy gently and then a little harder. Peggy pushed back. They both laughed, trying to make each other land on the overstuffed burgundy sofa.

Peggy defended herself by wiggling two fingers down the décolletage of Liane's latex dress, into the moist cleft between her girlish breasts. The dress itself resisted Peggy's fingers like a suit of armor.

Liane squirmed out of Peggy's grip and landed a good slap on her behind, wanting Peggy to feel it under the tight denim that covered her cheeks. Peggy squealed and tried to retaliate. Both women fell together onto the sofa, which held them like quicksand.

Wrestling turned into kissing as Liane lay atop Peggy, one of her knees wedged between Peggy's thighs, tormenting her wet slit. "Scared?" asked Liane, nibbling Peggy's earlobe.

"Not of you!"

Liane grinned and unbuttoned Peggy's blouse from the top down, exposing generous breasts spilling out of her flower-print cotton bra. Liane wrapped her arms around Peggy to reach the bra-hooks at her back. With a quick pull, she slid the straps off Peggy's shoulders, releasing her hard red nipples to the air.

Peggy wouldn't look her in the eyes, but the embarrassment of exposure was clearly heightening her arousal. Liane bent down like a pecking bird to give each of her nipples a quick kiss.

Liane could see beads of sweat shimmering on Peggy's face and upper chest in a shaft of light from the window. Peggy's breath blew strands of Liane's hair away from her neck. "I could stop," offered Liane. "Just tell me when."

Peggy moved steadily against Liane's hard knee, rocking her clit rhythmically against it. Peggy's jeans and Liane's sheer tights added texture and friction. Liane suspected that Peggy was close to losing control.

"Don't—stop." Peggy's breathy voice caressed Liane's ears. Peggy grabbed Liane's nearest hand with its dangerous-looking black claws, and brought them to the soaked denim at her crotch.

Liane laughed softly and pulled down the zipper of Peggy's jeans. Then she held the sturdy fabric and helped as Peggy shimmied to free herself from her clothing. Liane imagined how she herself must look in her slick dress and masklike makeup, seducing a naked, breathless woman whose clothing lay scattered on the floor. Liane wondered if a superstitious Christian would mistake her for the Scarlet Whore of Babylon, or at least see her as evidence that a reign of appalling perversity was on its way. She certainly hoped so.

Peggy seemed to read her mind. "Frank," she huffed, "can go to hell."

Liane smiled down at Peggy's moving, womanly flesh. "He can go there with no help from us. Is that all you want?"

Peggy groaned as if her cunt would die of starvation if it wasn't fed soon. "Do it, Liane! What you—told me about."

"Mm. You'll be spoiled for anything else, babe." Liane reached for the purse that she had dropped on the low coffee table. Her slim, clawed fingers dug into jingling chaos, and emerged holding a small metal vibrator.

Peggy spread her legs apart, reaching for Liane. The svelte woman in the slick dress stuck her tongue out between red lips and licked at the slit covered in damp, curly, rust-colored hair. With one hand, Liane gently opened Peggy's lower lips, and used the tip of her tongue to probe Peggy's swollen clit.

"Aaohhh," moaned Peggy.

"Feel like a lesbian yet?" taunted the seductress. She turned on the vibrator at medium speed, and guided it into a slick, fragrant center. While aiming for Peggy's G-spot, Liane lowered her face to Peggy's clit and sucked it into her mouth. She used her tongue to mimic the rhythm of the vibrator in its new home.

Peggy made sounds that Liane had never heard from her before. She erupted like a geyser, gushing hot liquid. She hung on to Liane as well as she could with trembling arms.

Afterward, Liane stroked Peggy's hair and kissed her mouth, feeling her heartbeat and her breathing slowing down to a normal rate. Liane was tempted to sing a lullaby, but she was too excited to fall asleep herself. Peggy snuggled against her like a puppy, and pulled Liane tighter against her every time the restless woman shifted position.

"You're one of us now." Liane spoke into the pink shell of Peggy's closest ear.

"That was amazing." Peggy lay sprawled like a boneless sea-creature.

"But you still haven't told me," persisted Liane. She imagined herself as Woman Warrior's nemesis in a video game, jumping with lightning speed in front of her, behind, or approaching from the side, whichever would give her the greatest advantage.

"What?" Peggy sounded as trusting as a child.

"What he did to you just before you left. The things you can't get out of your mind. I bet you couldn't believe he would really go that far after he had seemed so nice. How he could just ignore you when you were saying no and please and stop it. How he could rip your clothes off when you weren't expecting it, and tell you it was all your fault. How he seemed like a totally different person, and you didn't know how to bring back the one who cared about you."

Peggy curled in on herself. "You seem to know it all, Liane. What do you want me to say?"

"What you're afraid of since then. Where you don't even want to touch yourself because it would bring back awful memories." Liane held Peggy from behind, breathing into her hot scalp.

Peggy turned her head awkwardly to make herself heard, but she wouldn't turn fully around to face her tormentor. "Okay, but promise you won't do it. I really don't want it, Liane."

"I promise, honey. I want to help you, not make it worse."

"He fucked me in the ass. That was his thing. The first time I actually let him because I didn't know how much it would hurt. After that, he wouldn't stop because he said I needed to get used to it, but I never did. There. Now are you happy?"

"Not happy that he hurt you, Peggy. Did he use lots of lube?"

"Just juice from my—you know."

"I bet he didn't spend lots of time warming you up, either, did he? Talking to your shy little rosebud and tickling it with a finger or a plug?"

Peggy snorted in dismissal.

Liane couldn't bear to stay in her clothes. "Wait a sec. I'm overdressed for this conversation."

She stood up to take off her dress. She felt marinated in her own sweat, and her skin needed to breathe.

Peggy watched over her shoulder as Liane peeled off her shiny outer shell. Liane hooked her thumbs into the waistband of her tights and rolled them down her legs along with her black lace panties.

Liane turned her back on Peggy, shook her behind, bent over, and looked at her from between her legs. She was flexible as an eel, and hoped her pose could hold the attention of a woman who was still recovering from a fabulous fuck and an ugly memory.

Peggy laughed, sat up, and opened her arms for Liane. The thin woman danced away to a corner hutch with wineglasses in it, glass behind glass. Light from the window bounced from one reflecting surface to the next as Liane made herself invisible by crouching down into shadows.

She opened a drawer and stood up, holding a tube. She came back to Peggy, grinning. "You wouldn't hurt me, would you, girlfriend?" Liane shook her dark, wavy hair over her shoulders as Peggy pulled her forward by the waist. "Can you guess what I want?"

Peggy looked interested but unsure.

"My turn, Peggy. I bet you could give it to me." Liane looked into Peggy's eyes, willing her to trust her own feelings. Peggy held her and gave her a long, slow kiss with lots of tongue.

Liane reluctantly pulled her mouth away to catch her breath. "This is lube," she explained, pushing it into the hand that reached for it. "It smoothes the way for all kinds of good stuff. You know where."

Peggy chuckled as if she could hardly believe her luck. She held Liane by the shoulders and used her tongue to leave a long wet snail-track from her collarbone to a point between her breasts, and then to each perky nipple.

Liane was impatient. "Sit here," she ordered, standing up. Then she spread herself luxuriously across Peggy's lap, her wet crotch pressing into Peggy's solid thighs, and her ass raised up in the moonlight.

"Ahh," sighed Liane. Her hips pumped steadily, working up a rhythm.

Peggy took the hint and reached between Liane's legs to find her clit. Peggy petted it with teasing gentleness. "You'll get it, honey," she promised. "On my terms."

Those terms were agreeable. Liane squirmed and sighed as Peggy tickled and stroked. "Nice ass." She raised one arm and slapped each of Liane's sassy cheeks. Peggy stroked the olive skin that showed a faint pink blush on each mound. Liane's puckered back opening felt the heat of Peggy's gaze before a finger massaged it. Cool, slick lube was patiently pushed inside. It eased the way for Peggy to challenge the ring of muscle and insert her finger beyond the first knuckle.

Liane could feel sparks radiating throughout her guts from the site of the delicious invasion. "Ohh, babe, don't stop. I'm yours."

Peggy's hands were hot and damp on Liane's lower cheeks. The finger spiraled deeper into a snug channel.

Peggy kept adding lube. She added another finger to explore Liane's depths. Liane moaned loudly enough to let the novice ass-fucker know that she was on—and in—the right track.

Liane was floating, but she knew she couldn't stay in that space for long. An explosion was overdue. Liane heard the buzz before she felt her own vibrator, on the lowest setting, being pushed steadily into her ass. She came hard, moving so wildly on Peggy's legs that she could barely be held in place. Peggy withdrew the magical toy, and held Liane until she stopped shaking.

Liane slid up, feeling open and liquid. It was the way she thought a mermaid would feel, gliding through the ocean. "Honey," she said, "you're so good. It's so good. I know you feel me." She could feel Peggy smiling.

Liane had lost count of the times she had met Peggy in the bar where danger hung in the air, brought her home, and had her way with her. Lesbian cherry-busting was still their favorite game, even now that Peggy's ex-husband was out of the picture. Liane hoped Frank was learning new games in prison.

Tonight, Peggy had found a new path, a dark tunnel with light at the end of it. Liane knew she would want to go back there again, and check out all the angles. Sweet.

THE OLDEST VIRGIN

Shain Everett

My cell phone vibrates. *You have an unread message*. It's ten o'clock on a Sunday night, and freezing outside, but not freezing enough to snow because this is San Francisco, so a half-assed gray rain lazily smears the bedroom window. I'm lying on my bed in my underwear, bored, tired of T-Bo and IMing. I'm wondering if my dad left any weed in his sock drawer before he fucked off to Hawaii with his girlfriend for two weeks. Wafts of warm air billow around my arm as I reach for my phone because I've jacked the heat in the apartment for days. *Who says I can't enjoy the tropics too, eh Pops?*

The message is only two words. *Come over*. Then an address somewhere in the Tenderloin. I go back a few screens to find out who it's from, pretending I don't already know.

You wouldn't guess by her name that everyone wants to bang Beverly. I mean, come on, *Beverly*? It's not exactly a hot name, not like *Van-ess-a*, which is so dripping you might as well be saying *Pus-sy*. Or *Anna* (sultry, with a little vroom-vroom to it), or even

Kate (straightforward fucking). *Beverly* is not easily whispered against someone's neck as the hot stars of your orgasm creep up from your toes and explode. But the minute you see her, Beverly, it stops being your grandma's middle name and becomes the sweetest, sexiest damn thing you've ever heard.

At least, that's what the guys that want to fuck her think, and there are lots of them. Or at least there were, when Beverly went to my high school. You should've seen them, the first day of school, circling her like oversexed apes: fresh meat! Beverly, she stood out, even I could see that, in the ever-swirling shit pot of our inner-city high school. First off, she was tiny—despite the towering heels of her fuck-me boots, only about five feet—but her perfectly proportioned body (perfect tits, tiny waist, bubble ass) made her look like a disturbingly erotic Bratz doll. Almond-shaped, gold-brown eyes, and Angelina Jolie lips without the collagen injections. Cap all that off with a sparkly diamond-stud nose piercing and a sheet of straight black hair down her back, and you know that everybody with a dick within a ten-mile radius was tripping over his hard-on.

But instead of gathering around the vending machine to discuss who would ask her to the prom, dudes at my high school got their kicks by getting high in their cars and cruising the lunch yard with baseball bats to watch everyone scatter: *Ha ha!* In other words, they were not exactly skilled at dating. Instead, some dudes sucked their teeth and hissed "*Mamacita,*" as she walked to the bathroom, and some called her a frosty bitch, and then left notes stuck in the gills of her locker with their MySpace addresses. Everybody else just stared. Beverly ignored them all, only looking long enough to deem them "boys," not like the "real men" she preferred to ball back in her old neighborhood.

At first she ignored me, too. Who wouldn't? I was just another mousy-haired chick with big tits, even if I did hide them under my sweatshirt. It wasn't until she figured out that I was a virgin that Beverly took any interest in me.

We sat next to each other in Dumb English for months without speaking. Or, rather, I sat with all the other girls in the great solar shadow she cast, imagining male hormones coating the classroom like an unseen, sticky fog. One day the teacher made us partner up to do some stupid worksheet on *Romeo and Juliet*. I hated Beverly just a little, like every other self-respecting, average-looking girl in the school did, so I was less than enthusiastic. Close as I was to her, I could smell the minty tang of her mouth as she worked her gum. Beverly heaved a sigh, not lifting her gaze from her cell phone, and demanded, "If I'm gonna *cut* myself, I'd at least wanna *get* something out of it. What is all this big deal shit about when they never even fucked?"

For a beat I blinked and said nothing. Then I realized she meant *Romeo and Juliet,* which I hadn't actually read, but everyone knows how that one turns out, right?

"Maybe they weren't interested," I said suddenly, surprising myself. Fucking dumb thing to say. I almost never talked at school, let alone to people that looked like Beverly.

"Not interested? In *fucking* each other?" Her eye-roll said, *How did I get stuck with the stupid girl?*

"Yeah." I was defensive now. "Maybe they just weren't interested."

Beverly looked hard at me as she slowly folded her arms around those angel tits of hers. I felt myself flush, but I stared back. I might have been a nobody, but I didn't take shit, either. Plus I bet every dude in that room would have killed to see Beverly in a catfight, hair askew, boobs swinging. She was either going to make a scene, or I was going to burst into flame. Then something shifted and I watched her eyes light up, her face splitting like ripe fruit into a wide grin. She threw back her head and laughed, a real cackle that bounced off the concrete walls of the classroom.

"Girl, you never got some, huh?" There was honey in her voice. "That's why you said that shit. You're a virgin."

It was true. Sort of. I was a virgin—in the way that she was thinking, anyway. And I had said that Romeo and Juliet weren't interested in fucking each other because I wasn't interested in balling any of the Barneys at our school. Who could blame me? But I sure as hell wasn't going to let on that Beverly was right.

"Fuck you." I said, trying to sound serious. But my feet felt like fish in my shoes. *Beverly,* the hottest chick in school, *is talking to me. Teasing me!* I felt a smile pulling at the corners of my mouth.

"Oh, shit. Don't be like that. It ain't my fault you're a virgin! Shit." I loved the way Beverly put about eight extra syllables in that last word.

The next moment was one I'd think back on later. Beverly's flashing eyes ran over me appraisingly. It was as if she said the words aloud before she asked me my name: *You'll do*. And from then on, strangely, we were, like, *friends*.

Okay, this is the part like in the movies where time passes, but you see it anyway in one long, pukey-puke happy action scene, where the characters do everything successfully and high-five each other a lot, all with an unnaturally peppy pop song in the background. But in my and Beverly's movie, we'd be doing shit like ditching school to hang out at her apartment, and hitting up old men who liked Beverly's rack to buy us vodka at the corner store. Then I'd go buy some chips and gum (Beverly never seemed to have any money). We'd get drunk in the stairwell at the Towers, or smoke out if I could score any weed, laughing our asses off and shivering in the fog. Then you'd see us crashing at my dad's, 'cause he's never there. We'd be talking in the dark, me sprawled on the bed with the spins and one foot on the ground, hoping she didn't see.

Beverly was so spectacularly self-centered, after a while she made *you* believe that you were missing out if you were not up to the minute on when she last took a crap. Guys wanted to fuck her shitless. Shit, *girls* wanted to fuck her shitless, but they'd settle for *being* her. A little of her fairy dust rubbed off on me, and suddenly girls that previously considered me a walking corpse said hello to me in the hall by name. *There's that girl that's friends with Beverly!* Maybe some (okay, *all*) of Beverly's appeal stemmed from the fact that she was undeniably the hottest chick any of us had ever seen. And, also undeniably, Beverly was absolutely obsessed with talking about sex.

Beverly was a veritable pornographic infomercial broadcasting 24/7. Missionary or doggy? Long or thick? Swallow or spit? Beverly had an answer to any erotic quandary, solicited or not, and loads (pardon the pun) of field experience. She talked for hours about who she'd had sex with (lots of hot, rich, well-hung guys back at her old school), how she'd done it (doggy, anal, but not with another girl, that would be skanky), and—who hadn't done it. Which, as you may've guessed, is where I came in.

Beverly was equally obsessed with the fact that I was, technically, a virgin. The fact that I'd never ridden some dude's salami was like a meteorite slamming into my face, lodging there, and me walking around school with it like it was no big deal (her analogy). Needless to say, it was a social handicap. Beverly told me she wasn't sure how long she could continue to be friends with someone so, well, *virginal*.

Thus began her quest to get me laid. Beverly was always talking about dudes that she'd been with, but that she'd be cool if I boned, "just to get you started." She would even march up to some crazy-ass stranger and ask if he wanted to bang me. I'd watch the guy's face melt in disappointment when I dragged her away (usually they thought she was pimping *herself*). She just laughed when I told her to shut up, as though my intact cherry were the funniest damn thing in the world.

"You're *eighteen*. You're the oldest damn virgin I know," she said so many times I lost count. "Like, by *a lot*."

I didn't mention that she was almost twenty, and still in high school. I laughed off all of her crazy shit. But after a while I realized I was never worried about my supposed virginity before Beverly; after Beverly, I started to wonder.

After a couple months of BFF, Beverly didn't show up at school when we'd planned to actually go to class, and she stopped picking up her cell. I saw her with some skinny-necked chick who was walking close enough to be her shadow. Giraffe Girl and Beverly were falling all over each other laughing the way we used to do. The message was loud and clear and so fucking "Dawson's Creek" I could've puked. I'd been replaced. Or maybe I had just been a stand-in all along. In any case, it sucked, but I made like I didn't care and went to class.

Later on I saw Beverly in Dumb English, and I decided to use my interpersonal skills. I walked up to her and asked her why she was being such a bitch.

"Fuck off," she said before she pushed past me. "And quit calling me."

We only talked to each other one more time, when I sent her a message: *Thanks for ditching me, bitch.*

She texted back immediately. *Whatever, VIRGIN.* The last word was all capitals and extra letters and took up half the screen. Then I wished I'd called her a slut instead.

Next semester, depending on who you heard it from, Beverly'd gone back to Oakland, or she was on crack, or she fucked the girls' basketball coach, whatever. The guys still had blue balls, and her legend lived on. I didn't hear shit from her.

Until now. The number is Beverly's, but I don't know the address.

Come over. And then an address.

She expects me to just jump? Fuck that. I don't write back. But I don't erase it, and I pretend not to notice that my heart is jangling like a pair of hoochie earrings. Feeling flushed, I get up and open the bedroom window, leaning over the sill to look down at the street below. The rain's slowed to a steady drip that after a minute plasters the hair to my neck. Ten minutes go by. My nipples curl tight into themselves, making me shiver in my panties and wifebeater. I close my eyes for a minute, filling my lungs deeply with wet air. I want a beer, just a stupid beer. Beverly would have liquor. She'd tip it back, watching my reaction, laughing with her eyes. But I'm not going over there. Fuck her.

I breathe out and open my eyes. It's just homeless dudes down on the street, taco-wrapped in colorless blankets, and Mexican couples herding sleepy children that bump into each other like moths. It's not her, watching me. I make myself admit that I'd been fantasizing it was her. It's not the first time.

Beverly would only call me for a reason, and I have a pretty good idea what it is. I close the window against the cold and stand looking out. After a while I realize I've stopped shaking. I'm so sober I feel drunk.

I leave the apartment fifteen minutes later.

I'm going to get laid.

* * *

It's stopped raining when I get off the MUNI, but I walk down the street she gave me a couple of times before I find the building. It's a mean-looking, concrete block of a thing, the color of skin. I scan the numbers on the stairwells until I find the right one. Beverly is somewhere in there, waiting for me, probably not alone.

I open the greasy glass door into the hallway to the stench of piss and cigarettes and climb the stairs, glad there's no one around. After scanning the numbers, I find the door and force myself to knock, loud. No one answers for what seems like an eternity. A flare of relief lights in my chest before it's extinguished by pride, because what the fuck is she playing if she's gonna call me all the way over here and not even answer the fucking door? I raise my fist to knock again and jump when the door suddenly thumps open, and two eyes peek out at me from behind the chain. Beverly's pupils dilate in the hallway light.

"Oh...you came." Her voice is blank.

"Yeah. Yeah, well, it's fucking cold out here. Are you gonna open the door?" But she's already closing it to undo the chain; then she cracks it, and I slip past her.

I look around the living room of the dark, boxlike apartment. I can tell right away it's not Beverly's place; no cute shoes on the floor, no makeup case the size of a small dog spewing out on the coffee table. Plus it smells distinctly like dude in here; a funky mix of sweat and testosterone and Top Ramen lingers in the air. I can't help wondering what Beverly's up to.

It's cold, but I take off my wet sweatshirt anyway, giving her a minute to check me out. Push-up bra under cut-off black T-shirt, big hoop earrings, mascara, all left in a heap on the bathroom floor by my dad's anorexic girlfriend. I've lost weight since Beverly last saw me, but the black pants still hug my ass. I feel like a cross between Miss America and a horny circus clown.

"Check you out, shit," she says in that telemarketer voice as her eyes slink over me. I detect a faint hint of approval.

She walks past me into the kitchen that's attached to the living room, and I drop onto the couch. Now it's my turn to check her out. The golden flesh of her love handles muffin-tops over the waistband of her sweatpants. The perfectly formed orbs of her ass jiggle under their personalized message to the world—*You Wish*—as she pours cheap gin and juice into a huge plastic cup. When she walks back into the living room, I can tell she's gained weight since the last time I saw her. Most girls would look like shit, but Beverly is a milk-fed cat, all sensuous curves and vacant eyes. She's never been hotter. I feel a liquid gold gathering in my panties that makes my face go red.

Curling up on the opposite side of the couch, she takes a long sip of the drink without offering me any. Now she's all sneaky kitten smiles and giggles.

"He wants to fuck a virgin." She lets the words hang there in the dank air of the apartment. She watches my face, no doubt relishing the drama. For a minute, I think I might actually do what I came here to do, which is call her a ho, smack her, *something* to make her feel bad for ditching me. Then we'll be friends again, once I fuck whatever guy she's got holed up in here. It's time. *The oldest virgin she knows.*

"Okay, whatever," I say, too quickly, and the corners of Beverly's smile tremble.

"Oh." It dawns on me that I've made it too easy for her. She'd wanted to have to convince me. "Well, anyway, at least you're finally gonna get *rid* of that shit."

She makes it sound like a case of crabs. I watch as Beverly grabs a chunk of her hair to examine the split ends, and fakes a yawn. I feel a sudden, hot surge of rage. Beverly doesn't care that I haven't seen her for almost a year. All she cares about is her stupid little power games. She hasn't changed at all. Slap a big fat *L* on my forehead: had I really come here hoping she wanted to be friends again? Fucking pitiful! I grab the cup from her hand, jostling her and spilling it.

"Jesus, lay off my shit, will you? God." I ignore her and chug it, feeling the sweetness and fire hit my stomach like a storm cloud. I suck in my breath and my brain shifts. I'm starting to think smacking that perfect face just won't do.

"So where is he? Let's get this shit going already." My voice sounds as forced as a radio announcer's. Beverly doesn't notice because she's picking spilled ice out of her luscious cleavage like a mother baboon.

"He's in the bedroom. He's totally into, like, me, but I told him what's up and he's gonna help you out because you're a..."

"What a guy." Luckily sarcasm requires higher thought, and thus is lost on Beverly. "But will you, um, come in there with me, just for a minute?" I'm going carefully to get this thing right. "I'm kinda nervous, and you're, like, so experienced."

Beverly smirks, and I know I've got her. It's only a minute until I'm following her down the dark hallway, loving the luscious cleavage of her ass peeking out the top of her sweatpants. It's hard to act like someone walking the plank. Beverly plays older sister, even goes so far as to tell me to make sure I move my hips so he'll come faster. It's a real Marsha and Jan moment.

My eyes take a minute to adjust in the dim light of the bedroom. Then I see him, sprawled out on the bed in his tighty-whities, his junk spilling out the sides. He's small and wiry and reminds me of a weasel with his pubelike goatee. I can't help but wonder where Beverly found him. The fact that he's undressed himself—*what an industrious young man*—makes me choke down nervous laughter. Cocky bastard. He barely looks me over as he grunts something unintelligible, maybe his name, his eyes already swinging to Beverly's tits. It's now or never.

I put my hand on Beverly's hip to stop her as she starts toward the door, looking pleased with herself.

"Hey, let's have some fun, huh? Like, all three of us?" I blaze a smile and push my face toward hers to nuzzle her neck, not letting myself notice yet the softness there, the hint of salt. The absolutely Beverly smell.

"Hey, get off, what are you playing at?" She jumps like I've bit her, but the dude's already off the bed with a paw on both our boobs, practically creaming his shorts. She slaps his hand away.

"Whoa there, killer," I say to him. "We've got all night." He jams his hard-on into my hip, tries to snake his arm around her wrist and pull us both toward the bed. But I'm ready for him.

"Hey, why don't you go get that bottle? We want to get messed up before we, uh, ride that thing."

Surprisingly, it works. He blinks at me, mumbles something about fucking the shit out of both of us bitches before he stumbles out the bedroom door. Which I promptly slam and lock behind him.

Beverly stands with her hands on her hips as I quickly strip off my T-shirt and jeans. "What the fuck are you doing?"

"Don't you want to play, Beverly? You like sex so much, why don't you fucking *have it* instead of talking about it all the time?" And I push her, not hard, but she doesn't expect it and she falls back onto the bed. I fall on top of her. She splutters and squawks.

"Relax," I grunt. "This will be the best yet. Believe me."

And she should. My cousin's best friend did, last summer when I was down in L.A. She believed it so much, she'd be pulling at my hair and stifling her screams with a pillow every night after my cousin fell asleep. And then it was her turn to breathe her hot breath through the fabric of my panties until I was half-crazed, until she took them off and made me come so hard I thought my head would pop off. Three times.

I tell Beverly this, slowly, and alternate slipping my tongue in her ear and probing the little pink hole with my tongue piercing. I hope she can hear me over the dude's pounding at the locked door. I ignore the racket, and with her squirming body under mine, I feel all my anger turn into a huge, warm wave of lust that makes me catch my breath. My fingers creep like ghosts to trace slow circles on her nipples through her tank top.

"I'm gonna kick your ass. Lemme up." Beverly says thickly, halfheartedly pushing my hands away.

"Tell me you want to," I say in her ear, my voice a far-off buzzing that feels separate from me. I clear my throat. "Tell me you want me to fuck you." My pussy is throbbing like a low-rider subwoofer. Long pause. For a moment I think I'll have to get up and leave, the whole thing's bust.

"Whatever," Beverly finally says. But her voice is a wilted flower on the side of the freeway. I can practically hear the pussy juice dribbling down her leg.

I sit up and move into position, straddling her waist. Next, the tank top: I pull it off her and her huge tits burst out like freed hostages. Entirely passive, she flops back down on the bed, stretching her arms above her head for me to catch and pin down against the covers while I rub my face in her breasts, licking and play-biting. My hands move across her stomach and hips, thumb the hard nuts of her nipples.

I sit up suddenly to undo the clasp of my bra and slide it off, wanting to feel her skin against mine. The pounding at the door has turned into a steady stream of pleas to be let in. Beverly stares at me like a stoned blow-up doll, saliva dotting the corners of her crumpled mouth.

"Take off your pants," I say quickly, impatient now. She complies, moving slowly as if through water, and pushes her sweats and thong to her ankles. I yank them off and there it is: the hottest pussy in town. A perfectly etched landing strip leading to petal lips. I can barely wait to taste her. Without taking her eyes off mine, she lets her knees fall open, a porn-star smile oozing across her face.

"Welcome to my jewel," she says, and laughs from deep in her throat. It's a practiced line.

"Don't give me any of that crap," I snap, and her eyes flicker but she doesn't say anything more.

"Touch your tits," I whisper to her, wanting to make her work for it. I nudge her belly with my knuckles when she doesn't move. She cups her perfect, tear-shaped breasts absentmindedly, her eyes fixed in space. I lower my head to her flat stomach, and then kiss the wide bowl of her hips. Slowly, slowly, entirely aware of her breathing, I go farther down. I lick a finger and work it deep into her cunt. She stiffens.

"Relax," I say. She stirs slightly and sighs, as though waking from a long nap. The pounding on the door has stopped: Weasel Boy has left the building. Her body unclenches inch by inch, melting into the mattress. I feel my insides ripening.

I move to pull on her labia, wanting to tease her, nibbling her musky lips. Her pussy has the smell of summer blacktop just after it rains: semisweet, with an undercurrent of metal, and something unnamable. I press my face into her clit, drumming a steady rhythm with my tongue piercing. Beverly begins almost imperceptibly to rock against it, pushing up into my mouth, asking for more. I quickly feed in another finger, and then another. A guttural sound escapes her throat.

When I sense that she's buzzing hot as electrical wires, I press my thumb against her anus, feeling the resistance and pushing past it. She gasps, and I hear her head thrash against the pillows. Slowly I bury my thumb in her ass, and Beverly moans in response. Her clit has hardened to a perfect pearl beneath the frenzied flicking of my tongue as I drive her on. My jaw aches almost as much as my pussy, which I'm dying to touch but I don't dare, not yet, not yet. Her rocking gives way to slow bucking, each thrust accompanied by a staccato of yeses that make Beverly sound like a deflating snake. She's close, her orgasm a fiery star of promise just below the horizon. I stop abruptly.

I raise my head to look at Beverly. Her beautiful face is a grimace of absolute pleasure, and she's gripping her tits like twin bazookas she's aiming to fire at my head. Her knees have gone typewriter, and a red map of Africa stands out on her chest. Her eyes are squinched shut, but as the cold air of my tongue's absence hits her cunt, they fly open.

"Don't stop," she stammers, staring right at me.

"Say please," I say, torturing her. I've never heard her use the word.

"Please...please!" She's panting like a desperate animal.

I want to shout with triumph, but I drop my head again to taste her pithy juice.

"And"—flick, pause—" that you're sorry"—flick-flick, longer pause—"for being such a bitch." I hover.

"I'm *sorry*," she cries, the words catching in her throat. "I'm so sorryyyy!"

My tongue is a zigzag of pleasure bearing down on her clit, pushing her over the edge. Her orgasm hurtles out of the darkness to explode within, the waves rolling over her as she lets loose a stream of dirty-ass, ecstatic cussing. I try to press into her as her body convulses again and again like a Sunday preacher who's just found the spirit. Finally, she collapses back on the bed, exhausted, to lie in her own juices.

I wipe my mouth, still tasting her, and climb up to lie next to her, both of us on our backs, breathing heavily, not touching. After a while I roll over on my side to face her.

"How's it feel?" I take her hand to suck on one of her Tootsie Roll fingers. Not that she'll need it when I get her to work on me; I'm already wet, wetter than I've ever been before.

"What?" Beverly is fuck-faced; her eyes make her look like Rip Van Winkle. But I can already tell she'll learn this shit quick. And be good at it.

A victorious smile creeps across my face.

"To not be a virgin anymore."

I AM NOT INTO WOMEN

Jacqueline Applebee

I am not, and I have never been, into women. I never experimented when I was in college, I never got so drunk that I accidentally kissed my female pals, and I never put on a show for any of my boyfriends as a special treat on their birthday.

But then I met Sheryl. Giggles were the soundtrack to her life. Every time I saw her, she was laughing about some silly thing or another. No one had the right to be that happy all the bloody time. Whenever I thought of her, and I seemed to think about her a lot, I could hear girly giggles in the background. It was like having voices in my head, but worse, because I knew I wasn't crazy—she was. There was no reason for any of this. I wasn't into women, and if I ever could be, it sure as hell wouldn't be a ginger-haired girl who thought that Hello Kitty was the most important thing in her life.

Everyone has an inner child, but Sheryl's redheaded child was right in my face. She worked two days a week at my office, and every time she came in, she brought sweeties to share. When she talked, especially when she stood close to me, her breath was aniseed twists, butter toffee, and chocolate caramels. Sheryl's desk was covered in little stuffed toys. Her computer desktop showed an image of a cartoon cat. This girl was unreal! How had she got through her interview for this job? I never used to be so bitter until Sheryl started working in the office. I felt undermined—all the men would laugh about her juvenile antics, and I began to worry that as the only other woman in the workplace, I would get lumped in with their view of her.

I started to avoid Sheryl, as I couldn't stand the constant childishness that made me feel stiff and awkward and...old. And that was the thing, really. She made me feel old, and I hated her for it. That jolly white girl didn't have a care. I was a working-class black woman, and I knew all the hurdles that stood in my path. My life was not all fun and games, and I was serious for good reason.

I was making a cup of tea one afternoon when she came into the small kitchen that the office used. I mentally sighed, and braced myself for another mindless conversation.

"What's that supposed to be?" She pointed at my arm, to the black tattoo that lay over the dark brown skin of my bicep. "It's a pretty star," she continued when I remained silent, desperately trying to ignore her.

"It's a snowflake," I said with gritted teeth. She raised an eyebrow and nodded, but then reached out and stroked her finger across it. I shivered right down to the soles of my feet, and Sheryl jerked away at my reaction in the same instant. We looked at each other, but the moment was broken as two guys from technical support walked in, chatting loudly. I was intensely grateful for their interruption—I am not into women, never had been, and I didn't want to start now. That went double for women who behaved like silly little girls.

If I had avoided Sheryl before, I was even more elusive afterward. I refused to believe the intensity of her touch had affected me so much. I gave my good friend and coworker Georgio a hand job after work on Friday evening in an attempt to exorcise Sheryl from my brain. I memorized the feel of his dick in my hand, wanting it to replace the feeling that Sheryl had elicited from me. I am not into women. I chanted the five words until they became my mantra.

I am not into women, but I couldn't stop thinking about her.

"I'm going to get a tattoo," Sheryl confided quietly to me one afternoon, as I washed my cup in the kitchen sink. I fought the urge to look around and check that she wasn't speaking to someone else. She pointed to her hip. "I want to have some little roses, here." I couldn't tear my eyes away from the spot on her skirt she had indicated. "Does it hurt?"

I counted to five before I replied, "It hurts like hell." Her pretty face fell, and I suddenly wanted to move heaven and earth to make her smile again. What was happening to me?

"Will you come with me?"

"What?"

"Will you come with me when I get my tattoo done? I'm a bit nervous about it."

I stared at her. Why was she asking me? I had done my best to avoid her, had never appeared friendly, never laughed along with her stupid behavior…I realized she was still smiling at me.

"Sure, why not?" I said, and she giggled and skipped away. I'm not joking, she actually skipped out of the room, and her ginger hair bounced with every hop she made. I was most definitely going crazy. I didn't do this sort of thing. I never did this sort of thing. I am not into women, least of all with some laughing girl-child.

Georgio had eaten something funny at lunch, and he spent

the rest of the afternoon throwing up out in the men's toilets. He mumbled something about a deadline as he dove for the restroom. I remembered that he had been working on a report that was due in the next morning. I shifted over to his desk, and eyed the scribbled notes in his scrawled handwriting. Georgio was a great guy, and my regular "friend-with-benefits," but right then, I wanted to hit him.

I had just shoved a huge stack of papers out of the way when Sheryl popped her head around the door. Her face took on a disappointed frown. "I'm sorry," I said, not daring to look at her any longer. "I'm snowed under."

She smiled tightly, and spun around without saying a word. It was the first time I'd known her to be silent. I was so glad when she left; my fascination with someone I didn't even like was starting to wear on my nerves. Compared to Sheryl, Georgio's incomprehensible report was bliss.

I didn't see Sheryl again until the next week. I was entering the ladies' toilets, and she was coming out. When she saw me, she grabbed my hand and yanked me into the nearest stall.

I am not into women. I am not into—oh god, she was saying something to me. Her glossy pink lips moved at an amazing speed.

"I did it!" she yelped excitedly, shuffling out of her tight jeans. I couldn't believe what she was doing, so I stood dumbly in the cramped space, transfixed by the private striptease I was being treated to. She giggled constantly as she disrobed, and at one stage, she had to pause and take a few deep breaths before she could continue. I was frozen in place while I tried to remember exactly what it was that I wasn't into.

Finally her too-tight jeans bunched around her knees, and I zeroed in on her white patterned knickers. Hello Kitty winked at me from a dozen different poses, and I suddenly felt like a dirty old woman. Sheryl pulled the elastic to the side, and that's when I saw her tattoo. A beautiful cluster of red and yellow rosebuds had been etched onto her pale skin in a loose bouquet. It was absolutely lovely. My finger reached out, and I drew a tip over the flesh that was warm and smooth. I looked up when I heard a hungry gasp, and was surprised at the big blue eyes that gazed down at me. I stepped away, feeling ashamed, seedy and sordid. I backed into the door, fumbling with the lock, but Sheryl's hand slammed it shut the second I had it open.

"I'm not a child," she breathed huskily.

"I never said you were." Where had all the air gone?

"I want you," she growled dangerously, and I started with fright. I'd heard of sexual predators before, and I'd foolishly assumed that they were only ever men. This playful kitty had suddenly turned into a lioness. There was no way she could be attracted to me. I was old enough to be her— She kissed me before I could get any further. In truth, I didn't know what else to say, apart from "I'm not into women," but at that moment, it seemed as if that was a lie. Her lips were the softest things I had ever felt, and her tongue was the most delicious morsel I had ever tasted. My mantra disappeared as Sheryl kissed me more.

"Don't be afraid," she said gently after she released me. Her hand reached to my blouse, and she slipped a finger over the buttons, expertly undoing them with a flick. I couldn't move as she reached inside my black bra and cupped a heavy brown breast. She tweaked a nipple so gently that I almost sobbed for more. No one had ever touched me like that before. Why had it taken me so long to get into women? I was approaching thirty, and this was my first experience. I wanted to scream with the injustice of it all, but my body had other plans.

Sheryl bent over and sucked my nipple into her mouth. Every drop of blood in my veins seemed to zoom in on that small piece of dark flesh, and I swear I felt it grow at least an inch. Why would I be afraid of this? It wasn't as if I were being devoured by a beautiful flame-haired creature of the night. My hands tangled in her fiery tresses as I drew her to me. She groaned at the action, and the tremors of her voice made my whole body reverberate. Somehow my fingers returned to her tattoo, but this time I slipped inside the band of her stupid knickers, and into the hot wet part of her.

My mind knew the anatomical names for a woman's genitals. I had studied a little biology when I was younger, but in the here and now, the words seemed cold. Vulva, clitoris, mons, and labia were clinical words for the wondrous heaven I found myself in.

"Cunt," I whispered. "Pussy."

"Yeah, that's me," Sheryl giggled against my breast, and this time when laughter overtook her, I joined in too. She pulled away from my tits, leaving me cold and wet, but I didn't care; I was knuckle-deep inside Sheryl's cunt, curling my fingers against a special place inside her. I was suddenly grateful for my biology lessons. The bump above my fingertips meant that I was now massaging her G-spot. The stuttering gasp meant that I was doing something very right. I felt her muscles clench and unclench around me, and it was unlike anything I had ever known.

I was now into women, quite literally so. I continued to work my fingers inside Sheryl, and she sighed when she came, and then giggled like a child. I somehow knew that I would never get tired of that noise.

Surprisingly strong hands pulled my fingers out of her cunt, and she held my sticky digits up to my face. I faltered for a moment as I stared at my glistening fingers. I had only gotten as far as "I'm not into..." when I took a breath, and then stuck my fingers into my mouth, licking and sucking every trace of her into me. Sheryl smiled, and kissed me once more. We swapped spit and her juices, a tangled mess that was anything but childish.

"You were right," she whispered against my neck. "The tattoo—it hurt like hell."

"Let me kiss it better?" I asked hopefully.

She stepped back a fraction, and I squatted down in the small space of the stall. I pressed my lips to her painted rosebuds, and then I licked over them. The sound of giggles rang out once more. I was officially into women, and I knew I'd be getting into this particular woman a whole lot more from now on. I stifled a chuckle, and kept on licking.

MUDDY WATERS

Kristina Wright

I was completely out of my element and scared out of my mind. Against my better judgment, I had foolishly fallen in lust with an outdoorsy girl with a taste for extreme sports, and after three months of tame dates, she'd insisted I try something *she* liked. So, instead of sitting in a coffee shop sipping double-shot espressos while discussing Molière, which would have been my preference, I was bouncing around in a Jeep that had once been bright yellow and was now mud brown. It was mud brown because we were driving—bouncing, more like it—through mud. It wasn't just the Jeep that was muddy. Becky looked like a spa treatment gone horribly wrong, and I could only imagine that I looked just as bad.

While I clung to the Jeep for dear life, fearing the flimsy seat belt was inadequate to the task of keeping me contained in the vehicle, Becky bounced and whooped like she was on a thrill ride, her once-blonde braids caked with mud. We were out in the country somewhere south of Baltimore, some place I'd never been and hadn't even known existed until Becky had brought me there along narrow back roads that gave way to gravel roads ending in wide open fields dotted with wildflowers and scrub brush. After a three-day summer rain, the fields were little more than one big mud pool, and Becky thought this was the greatest thing in the world. Which made me question her sanity—and mine, for going along with this.

"Isn't this freakin' awesome, Kate?" she yelled over the sound of the engine and the wind whipping through the open Jeep as she made donuts in a particularly deep mud bog. "Man, I've missed muddin'!"

I forced a smile and was rewarded with a splatter of mud across my teeth. "Oh yeah, it's great," I shrieked, hoping that was a bit of rock between my teeth and not a bug. "Don't know why we didn't do this sooner."

Becky ran the Jeep up a slight incline and we went flying over it into another mud bog at the edge of a stand of trees. My stomach lurched and I closed my eyes, which only seemed to make it worse. Coming out hadn't been all that big a deal for me, but I had never imagined coming out quite this far for love.

"You okay?" she said, bringing the Jeep to a stop. "You look kind of green."

With my eyes still closed, I nodded slightly. "Fine, fine. Just a little queasy."

She patted my arm. "You'll be okay. You just need to get out and stretch your legs. C'mon!"

I groaned as I struggled out of the Jeep. I hoped she wasn't planning on taking me on a thirty-mile hike through the woods. Standing next to the Jeep, I bent over and took some deep breaths. All I could smell was the earthy aroma of mud—not a pleasant smell.

Becky was messing around at the back of the Jeep and

singing "Sweet Home Alabama," when I finally was able to get my stomach to agree not to discharge its contents. I watched as she removed a cooler from a webbed cargo net, along with a rolled blanket. My heart leapt—it didn't look like we were going hiking at all! There was a goddess!

"Thirsty?" she asked, holding out a partially frozen liter-sized bottle of water. "I've got power bars, too."

"Always prepared," I muttered, taking the water. "I don't suppose you've got a beer in there. Or a bottle of tequila?"

She laughed and gave me a one-armed hug as she chugged from another water bottle. "You're so cute. Such a city girl."

Despite the grungy state we were in, she kissed me. I tasted the cold of the water and the slight gritty texture of mud that was smeared on both our mouths. I pulled away and wiped my mouth with an even dirtier hand. "Yes. City girl. City girl needs shower before she makes out."

"No running water out here, but I think I can help." She pulled a large barrel-shaped thermos from the back of the Jeep. "Strip down. I'll give you a bath."

"Are you nuts?" I looked around. "I'm not taking my clothes off out here."

Becky laughed again. "Fine. If you won't, I will."

She set the thermos of water on the ground and quickly stripped out of her denim cutoffs and T-shirt. Her underwear, a simple white cotton thong, was the last to go. She looked incongruous standing there next to the muddy Jeep wearing only a pair of sneakers, with mud splatters marking her body like tan lines. Incongruous—and sexy as hell.

"Well?" She gestured toward the water jug. "Want to get cleaned up or want to stay muddy?"

What I wanted, quite suddenly, was to kiss her again. I quickly pressed her up against the Jeep, pulling her sun-warmed body against mine as I kissed her. I could still taste the mud, but the taste seemed like a part of her now, this earth-goddess chick of mine. She hooked her leg around my hip and pulled me into her, kissing me hard. I could tell by the way she was grinding against me that she was as hot as I was.

"Let's go home," I murmured against her open mouth.

Becky had other ideas. "Get naked."

"No."

She reached between us, palming my crotch. "C'mon. I'll spread the blanket out, and we'll fuck like bunnies."

The idea was tempting, even to a city girl like me. I thrust my pelvis at her, tweaking her dark nipples. "I'm filthy."

"So am I."

She had a point. I was too hot to argue anymore. Within moments, my clothes were piled on top of hers. I ran a hand through my short hair, feeling the drying mud that had caked it into spikes. I felt like something out of *National Geographic*, only in Born sandals, but it no longer seemed to matter. Becky was spreading the blanket out on the ground, teasing me as she bent over.

"Want to clean up now—or later?" she asked, a little breathless.

I eyed her, taking in her lean, tan body. "Later. It looks like all my favorite parts are mud-free."

She giggled as I tumbled her down onto the blanket. She wrapped her legs around my hips and pushed her pussy against me. She felt warm and smelled earthy, and I could feel myself responding to her. I anchored my hands under her ass and ground against her, lining my crotch up against her pussy. The hard ground was unyielding against my elbows and knees, but Becky's body felt too damned good to complain.

She moved against me, thrusting up so hard I knew we'd both

have bruises to show for it. I leaned down and sucked one dark nipple into my mouth, savoring the silky, sweaty taste of her skin. She moaned and clutched at my head as I sucked harder. I moved to the other nipple and gave it the same rough treatment, knowing it would drive her higher.

I shifted, moving one hand from under her to cup her pussy. She was lean and angular everywhere else, but here she was lush and soft, liquid heat coating my palm as I slid two fingers inside her. She gasped and arched off the blanket, and my fingers went deeper.

"Oh yeah," she moaned. "Fuck me, Kate."

And I did. Moving so that I was kneeling above her, I slowly withdrew my fingers and pushed them back inside her, again and again, until my entire hand was coated in her wetness. She spread her thighs wide, with her knees bent, and I loved the way her body opened to me. She gripped the blanket in her hands as she thrust up to meet my fingers. Her soft whimpers deepened to guttural moans as I stroked her fast and hard, her pussy tight around my fingers. She came quickly, clenching her thighs around my hand and pulling her knees to her chest. Completely still, the only thing I could feel was the quiver deep in her cunt that was almost like a heartbeat against my fingertips.

"That's it," I said, as I coaxed her through her orgasm. "Come for me, baby."

Her moans tapered away to soft gasps. I slowly withdrew my fingers, smiling at her. Quicker than I would have expected postorgasm, she grabbed me and flipped me over onto my back. I groaned as my shoulder blades came into contact with the hard ground, but I didn't dissuade her.

"My turn," she said, a wicked gleam in her green eyes.

She shimmied down my body until she lay between my spread legs. Then she opened my pussy with her fingers, and I felt the firm tip of her tongue against my clit. That one small sensation nearly brought me off the ground. I waited, expecting more, but that was all she was offering. Just the tip of her tongue on the tip of my clit.

Groaning in frustration, I reached out to find her mud-caked braids and gave them a tug. "More," I demanded.

"Yeah?"

"Yeah."

She ran her fingertips along the insides of my thighs. "But we're outside," she teased. "What if someone sees us?"

I nearly growled. "I don't care. Lick me. Now."

"Demanding wench."

I gave her braids another tug. "You have no idea."

I felt the tip of her tongue again, circling around my clit, dipping into my pussy, tasting my lips. I wriggled against her evasive tongue, craving so much more. The sun felt hot against my naked body, while the smell of mud and wildflowers was overpowered by the scent of sex. I tilted my hips up and found home. Becky slid her tongue inside my pussy and then lapped at my clit with broad, shiver-inducing strokes. I groaned and rocked against her tongue, her braids still clenched in my hands like reins.

She moaned open-mouthed against my pussy and I trembled, not only from the sensation of the vibrations through my sensitive clit, but at the thought that going down on me turned her on. Hot tears pricked my eyes suddenly, some well of emotion opening up as I rode her mouth. I was close, so close, and she somehow sensed it because she sucked my clit between her lips and flicked it with the tip of her tongue. One, two, three and I was coming into her mouth in a gush of wetness. I heard someone scream and realized it was me, my voice a wild wail as I rocked against the source of my intense pleasure.

She slipped her tongue inside my pussy again, her upper lip pressing against my quivering clit as my body tensed with waves of pleasure. I closed my eyes, feeling the tears trickle out while physical pleasure combined with an emotional release so intense it seemed as if I would never stop coming.

Finally, with every muscle in my body exhausted from the effort, I gasped, "Stop, stop! I can't take any more."

She stopped moving her mouth against me, but didn't pull away—probably because I still clung to her hair, which had come undone in my hands. With her mouth resting against my still-throbbing pussy, I stared up into blue, blue sky that seemed so much closer than I remembered.

I sighed as I released my death grip on her hair. She wriggled up beside me on the narrow blanket and grinned. "That was nice," she said simply.

"Your mouth is all wet." I leaned over and kissed her, tasting myself more than the mud that still flaked on her cheeks. "And you taste like me."

She ran her tongue over her shiny lips and giggled. "You should see the blanket. You've got a mud puddle under you."

"If you'd told me that was going to happen, I would have come mudding with you a long time ago." I wrapped my arms around her and held her close, the combined scent of sex and mud forever burned into my memory in the best possible way. "I could get used to this outdoorsy stuff."

Sighing contentedly, she nuzzled against my neck. "It's all in how it's presented."

She was absolutely right.

WINE-DARK KISSES

Catherine Lundoff

I knew what Janeece's lips would taste like, even back before I kissed her for the first time or had anything to compare them to except what I imagined.

We were the only women of color in our nine A.M. history class, both of us mixed race or whatever they're calling it now. My parents weren't big on terminology. It took me years to get my mom to even admit that I was adopted, and then I couldn't get much more than that out of her.

It wasn't like I didn't know I was different. I didn't look like anyone else at my school in the town where I grew up, and as near as I could tell, I didn't think like them either. I decided to be the only goth in town, for one thing. And I broke up with the most popular guy in school just before prom for another. All of my friends and most of my enemies thought I was crazy. I had plenty of the latter.

They were probably right. I didn't know why I had done it either, at least not until my first period history class at State.

"Hi. Looks like it's just you and me, girlfriend."

The word *voluptuous* had only been a polite way to say *fat* as far as I was concerned, until that morning. The girl who sat down next to me wore clothes that strained at her curves, hugged and revealed her breasts, her thighs. Just looking at her made me shiver all over, deep down inside.

I sat there, all black eyeliner and metal studs and black clothes, and said the first dumb thing that popped into my head. "Just you and me?" It was better than sitting there with my mouth open. Right then, I wanted anything but for it to be just her and me. The thought made me squirm with sheer terror.

The other girl looked me over as a slow smile parted her full lips. "You auditioning for a Marilyn Manson video?" She held out a hand at my scowl. "I'm Janeece. And yes, I'm always in your face."

I thought about telling her to fuck off and get her disturbing body away from me. But instead I took her hand, carefully as if it were a snake that might bite me, and responded, "Ingrid Peterson." I waited for the reaction that always followed.

Janeece gave me a long, considering stare. "Huh," was the only thing she said.

Then class started and we didn't talk again until it was over. By then I was watching her from the corner of my eye, entranced, captivated, horrified. It wasn't like I'd never had weird feelings about other girls before, but I'd always chalked it up to being a misfit. Here, I could remake myself and leave all the stuff I didn't like behind me, back in the small town where I grew up. And yet those stupid weird feelings were still there.

Janeece turned around as though she could hear my thoughts. "Got another class. See you on Wednesday, Ingrid." She managed to say my name like it wasn't a strange taste on her full lips, and I thought that I could listen to her say my name a whole lot more. I nodded, watched her walk away, and imagined...something. I didn't know what, really, I just knew that watching her move made me wetter than the most popular guy in high school ever had.

It was like that seeing her walk in on Wednesday morning, too. Here it was only our second full week of college and she was nodding and saying hi to a couple of people on her way over to me. Somehow it figured that she'd already made friends. I had managed to meet absolutely no one except my roommate. And Janeece. My stomach did a slow, leisurely flip.

We had a few minutes to kill so she asked the question I knew was coming—except it wasn't the one I expected. "You want to grab a coffee after class, Ingrid?"

I nodded, not trusting whatever would worm its way out of my black-lipstick-covered mouth. I have no idea what the professor said after that. If it turned up on an exam, I was doomed, but there was no way I could bring myself to care. I was having coffee with Janeece.

The glow lasted right up until I got my espresso and sat down across from her. She glanced at what I was having and grinned. "It suits you," was all she said. She sipped her cappuccino before she launched into small talk. I went along for the ride because I wanted to know more about her but didn't know how to get there without help.

Finally, she started to ask what I knew she'd ask eventually. "So, this is none of my business..."

"Yes, I'm adopted. No, I don't really know what I am. And no, I don't care." I crossed my arms over my black T-shirt and gave her my most ferocious scowl.

"I was going to ask if you had a boyfriend. Girlfriend. Whatever. But okay. I've got other friends who are transracial adoptees. Wherever you're at is cool by me." She leaned back and took another sip from her coffee. "You want to talk about it?"

I think that might have been when I fell into something like love. I spent a few seconds staring at her with my mouth open before it all started pouring out of me. Everything I wanted to tell someone who'd even kind of understand what it was like being the only one like me for years and years. I even told her about how my mom cried when she finally admitted I was adopted. And how my dad told me I was the light of their lives. Right before he asked me to never mention it again. I figured I could go nuts wondering where I'd come from and what my background was, or I could roll with it.

And I had, right up until now. Janeece's skin was darker than mine but not by much. Her hair was curly while mine was long and black and straight, and my eyes tilted up a lot more than hers did. Apart from that, it was like I had a mirror to look at, sort of. No more comparisons with white, freckled skin and long blonde hair. It was a beautiful moment.

She seemed to get it too, which made it all worthwhile. I talked until I ran out of words. It felt like forever but probably didn't go on for more than twenty minutes. Then this guy showed up just as I stopped talking. A gigantic god of a guy, the kind they put on college recruitment brochures. "Hi baby." He leaned over and kissed Janeece. "I'm just grabbing a coffee before class."

Janeece looked up at him and glowed. I wanted to crawl away under a big rock, dragging my crush and my ego and my words with me. Then she remembered I was there. "Hey Ingrid, this is Tony." She stopped there like that was all that needed to be said.

I looked up at the cocoa-colored hand being held out to me like I might bite it. Fortunately, someone who wasn't me took over and shook it gingerly instead of chomping down. “Hi. I should probably get going. See you Friday, Janeece?” Whoever that other person was got me the hell out of there to someplace quiet where I could snivel in peace. I cried my eyes out in a deserted bathroom for about ten minutes and then I was done. Sure, I might think about her again from time to time when I was getting myself off under the blankets at night. But I was done. I knew that was it.

Until Friday rolled around. This time when she walked into class, I was nonchalant. I even picked up my phone and made it look like I was texting as she dropped into the seat next to me. “Hey, Ingrid. Sorry we didn’t get to finish talking the other day. I didn’t realize you had another class then.” For the first time, Janeece sounded uncertain.

I shrugged, determined to seem like I didn’t care. “So how long you been with that guy? What’s his name again? Tony?”

Janeece raised one delicate eyebrow. “Nearly a year. We met before I got here, back when I was a senior and he was a freshman at State.”

“Yeah? He got a thing for jailbait?” It was the bitchiest thing I could think of to say, and I would have said anything to push her away right then.

It looked like it was going to work. Janeece scowled at me, and those luscious lips parted to let me have it just as the T.A. called our attention to the front of the room. “Later,” she mouthed at me. And that was that. Another history class I had no memory of. Good thing I was getting better at taking notes in a fog.

Class ended way too soon. Janeece whipped around in her seat and glared at me. “I don’t know why you’re being such a bitch about Tony. It’s not like you even know him. Or me either.” She gathered her stuff, throwing it into her bag at full force.

I sat there until she actually stood up to walk out of my life, just sat there looking at her and feeling my heart race. Then I dragged some words up from somewhere in my little reptile brain. "Look, I'm sorry. It just slipped out. I wasn't thinking." Score one for social skills.

Janeece looked over at me, still scowling. I tried to look contrite, not like that was easy while wearing black lipstick and a spiked wristband. "Well…okay," she said finally, and my heart started beating again. Meantime, I started spinning up a new fantasy. After all, just because she had a boyfriend didn't mean that chicks were totally out of the question—even one like me.

That was what triggered the next thing out of my mouth. "Wanna hang this weekend? You know, maybe study or go to a movie or something?" I said it in my tough-girl voice. No way was I going all romance novel and After-School Special in front of her. No matter how much I wanted to.

Janeece looked like she was thinking about it, but I think she'd already decided what she was going to say. "Could. How about coffee on Saturday? Here's my number." Then she met my eyes, and I just melted inside. Hell, all over my chair. For one horrible moment, I thought I was dripping down to puddle on the lecture room floor. Somehow I got through exchanging phone numbers and said 'bye until the next day. Somehow I got to my next class, and then my part-time job at the mall to work my shift.

I suppose I must have slept too, but the next thing I can remember is sitting across the table from Janeece at some cheap greasy spoon near the U. I watched every sliver of food go into her mouth and wished that it could be me that those lips closed around. I had it bad. But I don't think she knew then, not really. She just reveled in the attention and tried to get me to talk more.

Then when it was time to go, we made plans to hang out and study on Thursday night. I walked down to the mall on air, and nothing, not the stupid girls giggling over the vibrators or their equally stupid boyfriends trying to look goth, dented my mood. Time flew by and history got to be my favorite class.

When the big day finally rolled around, Janeece opened the door and stood aside when I showed up. She was wearing this amazing shirt that showed more cleavage than I'd ever dare to. I made myself not get all gross and drooly, but it took everything I had. Instead I was all slick and like, "Whoa, that's some shirt." Only I hate talking like that because it makes me sound like a moron.

She grinned at me. "Tony's coming over later."

Of course he was. My mood hit rock bottom. "Well, maybe I should take off..." I mumbled as she grabbed my arm and dragged me inside. After that, it was all lust and history until I couldn't take it anymore. "Gotta go crash, my friend. See you this weekend?" For an answer, she hugged me.

Now this wasn't just any hug, not like I'm an expert or anything. But still. It was the full-body clench, her breasts pressing mine down, her hips against mine. I almost kissed her neck, right where her soft brown skin hovered just beneath my lips. Somehow, I made myself stop and walk away.

Then back again that weekend. Lather, rinse, repeat for a few weeks until midterms were looming. This time when I went over on a Thursday night, Tony wasn't coming over later. In fact, if Tony was messing with the cheerleader Janeece thought he was messing with, Big T was out of the picture. She wiped a tear from the corner of one ebony eye, and I reached out and patted her shoulder awkwardly. Truthfully, I was torn between being pissed at him for hurting her and not quite believing it. I was no expert on relationships either, but T seemed pretty into her. It didn't seem too likely that he wouldn't be back and that she wouldn't take him back when he showed up.

Not that the thought was enough to warn me away. If he was out, maybe I had a shot right now. I'd had a few months since the beginning of the semester to research the whole girl-on-girl action thing, and I thought I might be ready. Now I just had to convince her of that, and since her roommate was over at her own boyfriend's room, tonight was the night.

I looked around and noticed the half-eaten candy bar on the nightstand and the two empty cans of Coke on the floor. Girlfriend was going for the sugar rush. She was grumbling about him now, on and on about how basketball had always been more important to him than she was. I leaned over and broke off a piece of the chocolate bar.

I started to put it in my mouth, but found myself looking at Janeece's lips instead. They were so rich and dark and soft, and I wanted to kiss them more than anything in the world. More than I wanted to be safe. More than I wanted to just be friends. I popped the chocolate in my mouth, leaned over, and kissed Janeece.

Anyone who tells you how hot a first kiss is when the other person isn't expecting it is trying to sell you some shit you don't need. Janeece froze and it was like kissing a blow-up doll or something. But she didn't pull away. Her lips were soft and sweet, and I wanted so much more. That was when it occurred to me that I was being an asshole, that maybe she didn't need her best bud hitting on her right now. I pulled away and braced myself for a slap or a yell that didn't come.

Instead she just looked at me, with those amazing lips parted in a slight pant. Her eyes looked wide and scared, kind of the way a horse does when it's really freaked out. I tried to figure out what to do next. If I played it cool like nothing had just happened, she might calm down, might forget it herself. But I didn't want to be forgotten, not now, not ever. I broke off another piece of chocolate and placed it between her lips.

There was a minute when time slowed down and stopped while she stared at me. Then it restarted when she lunged at me and kissed me back, her lips pressed around the chocolate. It was sticky, fumbling, and unbearably sweet. I could feel myself shake as I carefully put my arms around her to pull her closer. Whatever happened next was all worth it, even if she threw me out and never talked to me again; even if I was afraid that she was just doing this to get back at Tony.

Her chocolate-covered tongue awkwardly probed between my lips, and it was like I'd been shocked by an electrical outlet or something. My stomach did flips, and I wet my pants between my trembling thighs. No, not that way, you perv! The good kind, or so I hoped. I had never felt like this before about anyone, and I was scared shitless about what would come next. Should I touch her? Would she touch me? I tried tilting down toward the bed, not a full drop but just kind of a hint. She pulled back, breaking off the kiss, and I froze.

Janeece gave me a long hard look. Then she reached out and started yanking my shirt out of my pants. I squawked like a duck or something and tried to keep it on, right up until she leaned over and pressed her lips on the little bit of my skin exposed above my belt. This time I groaned. She ran her tongue over my belly and I fell back on the pillows.

She grinned and pulled my shirt up farther. She was nipping at me now, her tongue and lips working their way over me until I was gasping for air. She loosened my belt and stuck her hand down the front of my jeans at the same time as she bit my nipple through my T-shirt. I bucked upward against her hand, trying to stop its advance by grabbing at her wrist, but it was too late. She had slipped past the line of defense provided by my underwear, and her fingers were slipping around in the soaking wet space between my legs.

I spread my legs wider, hoping that she'd know what to do, that she knew how to find the spot and the motion that would make me let go. "Shit, girl," she murmured against my boob. "You are so wet. All that for me?" I nodded as my hips moved involuntarily, rocking against her hand even though she was nowhere near where she needed to be.

I grabbed at her shirt with my free hand, tugging at the buttons until they pulled apart, spilling her beautiful breasts out into my completely unworthy hands. I squeezed one, flicking her nipple with my thumb, and she groaned deep in her throat, head tilted back, eyes shut. In response, she stuffed two fingers inside me and my back arched, straining against her.

Somehow, I managed to pull one of her breasts free of her bra, kneading it like bread in my desperate grasp. She pulled her hand free of my jeans, and I whimpered like a puppy until I realized that she was going to take off her blouse and bra. I sat up and yanked mine off too. Then I reached for her, pressing her warm brown skin against mine, smooshing our boobs together while I kissed her as hard as I could. Her thigh landed between my legs and I rocked against it, letting the seam of my jeans find my clit. With my free hand, I reached behind the waistband of her skirt, stuffing my fingers down in the thick forest of hair between her legs.

Now we were both moaning, sucking on each other's tongues like candy, licking the last bit of chocolate from each other's lips. I could feel her wetness now and I wanted to taste her, wanted to feel her come on my tongue. I twisted around so she was underneath me and started kissing my way down to her skirt. She raised her hips and let me slide it off, pulling her underwear off with it. I buried my face in her fur, licking at the wetness I found beneath it like I'd been doing it all my life.

My first two fingers found their way inside her, and she

thrust against my face with a yelp. I shifted my tongue to where I thought her clit would be and started licking my way around in small circles. My fingers moved inside her like they knew what to do, and Janeece rocked and moaned, her thighs stiffening around my ears. I was in heaven now, and I knew what I wanted. She tasted like nectar, some combination of cocoa butter and guava.

I guessed I was doing this right from her reaction, or at least I hoped so. I sucked at her skin, feeling something harden slightly under the pressure, and she came, clawing at the pillows and groaning louder than I would have dared to. I would have kept going but she pulled away, dragging me up to her mouth to kiss her.

Then her hand was back down inside my jeans, her fingers probing for and then finding my clit. She rubbed for a minute, maybe less, and I came hard. My back arched and my eyes closed, mouth straining to stay shut over the yell I wanted to give.

Then it was all whispered sweetness, soft skin on skin touching and feeling and all that girl stuff I'd been dreaming of since I met her. She never said she loved me, and I didn't say it either, not sure that I should let the thought out. Maybe I didn't. I'd never been in love before, after all. Maybe this wasn't it.

I was on a little cloud of pure joy—right up until Janeece's roommate, Lisa, unlocked the door. She stood there, staring at us, mouth open in shock and horror as we rolled off the bed to grab our clothes.

I felt a little better once I was covered up, at least until I saw Janeece's face. She wasn't looking at me or Lisa. Instead she was staring at her desk. I glanced over and found myself looking at a big framed photo of her and Big T, and I went cold all over.

Janeece's shoulders were stiff, and her face was closed off. I guessed then at what would happen next. Maybe I could have done something about it right then, but I didn't know what.

Instead I got mad. I looked up at her roommate, who had finally closed her mouth and was backing out of the doorway. That was it.

"You already saw. Why leave now?" I snarled as I slipped my spikes back on and my courage with them.

Janeece shuddered all over. "She didn't see a goddamn thing," she whispered, her voice hoarse and angry and cold. "Not a goddamn thing. Did you, Lisa?"

Lisa looked from her to me and shook her head. Janeece looked at me finally. "Guess we're done studying." Her voice came from somewhere far away, and her eyes were like stone.

My stomach dropped down a few floors, and I clutched at a chair for balance. She was kicking me out of her life, just like that. I could feel the tears coming on, but there was no way I was going to cry, not in front of them. I found what was left of my voice. "And I guess you satisfied your curiosity about that, huh?" I grabbed my shoes off the floor and shoved my way out past Lisa.

I put the shoes on once I got to the stairwell, and then took the steps two at a time. I still didn't cry, not until I got back to my room. Then I buried my face under my pillow so my roommate wouldn't hear.

Janeece didn't show up for history again after that, but I made myself stay in the class anyway. Once I was able to do that, I dragged my miserable numb self out to meet the other local goths and queers and adoptees, and slowly and painfully, I found a community of misfits like myself. Then after a while, I wasn't miserable at all, *or* numb.

Janeece and I avoided each other at first, leaving the room whenever the other one showed up and all that dumb crap you do when stuff like this happens. I dreamt about her for a while but eventually that stopped too. After spring break we even got to being able to say hi to each other, sort of.

I saw Janeece during finals week of our freshman year, and she was sitting with Tony in the quad. I guessed they were back together, but it didn't bother me as much as it would have a few weeks back. They both surprised me by nodding and smiling in my general direction, and I sort of waved back, but I didn't go over. Janeece and I might get to be friends eventually, but I wasn't ready for it yet. I didn't know that I ever would be, honestly.

Besides, that same day I had a date with a hot girl from my art class, and she was waiting in the coffee shop for me. I could feel the butterflies dancing in my stomach. I thought about kisses like wine from someone who felt the way I did, and I smiled as I opened the door.

FEMME INTO ME

Maggie Cee

She fucked the femme into me. I know I'm not supposed to say this, but it's true. I'm supposed to tell you about how it's always been there, from the beginning, and in a way it was. You can see it in the pictures, four years old in a tutu, playing with the bicycle pump; eight years old at Easter, head inclined, pink dress with a wide lace collar. Then thirteen, fourteen, skirts, long skirts, lots of layers, not sure how to be a girl without being frivolous or silly, not sure how to live in my girl body, always too hard or too soft.

She drew it out with her hand inside me, with her weight on top of me, with her eyes on me. She loved my girl body, loved my ass in tight jeans, my legs in skirts.

She fucked the femme into me.

Or out of me, I'm not sure. *Into* implies that it wasn't there to begin with, and *out of* implies that afterward, it was gone. Neither is really quite right. And we weren't just discovering my femme, we were becoming butch and femme together, top and bottom, daddy and girl.

She had a brilliant smile and short hair swept in a dozen directions, big belt buckles and a walk like a confident twelve-year-old boy.

On our third date, I wore a skirt: long black jersey, almost indistinguishable from pants. I wore skirts all the time to class and parties and performances, but she was a real dyke and I was nervous that she'd think me straight or uncool. She said later she didn't even notice until we were kissing on my dorm room bunk bed, and she slid her hands up my legs, pushing the skirt up to my hips. She said, "I love skirts," with a sexy foolish grin, and something inside of me uncoiled, released.

She fucked the femme into me.

She'd never dated a girl like me before; her girlfriends had been snowboarders and hockey players like her, with strong shoulders and low centers of gravity. She'd never dated a girl with long hair, but she loved it, wanted me to wear it down, stealing my elastics and refusing to give them back unless I bartered sexual favors. I wanted it up off my face, but I learned to do it for her, learned not to care if the ends frizzed all over the place. She ran her fingers through my hair, pulled me to her, and I filled with melting water and desire.

She fucked the femme into me.

She was a sculptor, and she needed a body. I told her she could cast me. On a warm spring afternoon I lay on my back on a tarp and let her cover my small breasts, the bird's wing of my collarbone, my outstretched arms. I watched her work, with small strips of plaster, dripping water; concentration on her face. Then we had to wait. She pulled my hair off my face, kissed me. I wanted to turn my face to her, but I lay still inside the cast.

My top half was cold, immobile. I was just a head, a pair of legs, a cunt, and she was undoing my jeans, she was touching me, my legs were becoming tangled with hers and she was sliding into me and everything was bright and sharp and hot. *This is it. This is it,* I thought.

See, I was eighteen and a virgin, with a much longer resume for queer activism than for sex, queer or otherwise. I'd spent years lusting after shaved-headed andro dykes, convinced that none of them would ever find me attractive.

She fucked the femme into me.

One night in her mother's house, in a tiny bedroom under the eaves, she kept me on my stomach. She'd fucked me from behind before, of course, but on this night she was so slow, so teasing, and we had to be so quiet. Thoughts of submission, of giving up control, began to bubble up in my head as she moved down my body with her maddening touch.

We ceased to exist in ordinary space, outside this room, this bed, this hour. Floating in a colorless ocean of sensation, balancing on the edge of orgasm for hours, I found myself on my back again. "Don't kiss me back," she said, "just let me have your mouth." I responded as if it were an order upon which my very life depended. At the very core of my being I let go, gave her my submission, my obedience, although I wouldn't have used those words.

A month later we were in a hostel outside DC, less than twelve hours before I would take a bus to Yellow Spring, West Virginia to work for three months. On the train down I'd read Stephen King to her and the *New York Times* to myself. She slid two fingers into me under my hippie skirt as New Jersey rolled past. She said, "I bet I can get my whole hand into you." The very thought made my cunt clench and expand.

She was teasing me on the thin hostel sheets, going so slowly, her mouth on my breasts, in the hollow between them, her fingers light on my hips and thighs. "Please." The thought echoed in my head for long minutes before I said it. Her mouth was on my clit, and I was sucking on her fingers, swirling my tongue. "Please." She looked up. "Please what?" For a moment I was suspended in silence, afraid that there would be no turning back, until my desire forced its way from my cunt, bubbling up to form words. "Please fuck me."

She moved up to take my hands, pinned them over my head, and I was gone, my body melting into the thin worn sheets as she leaned her weight into me. I was nothing, I was nerve endings and cunt and muscle and wetness and bone, I was hers.

I arched my back and saw something lushly green and tropical rustling in the humid breeze outside the open window. I thought, *I will never forget this.*

Later she looked up at me, her light blue eyes sharp, and said, "You were very good. I'll have to be harder on you next time." Years later, after canes and wax and knives and play parties, after the devastating end of that relationship and the beginnings and endings of many others, those words still echo in my cunt.

I would have sworn she put her fist into me, but those big sculptor hands never fit all the way inside me. She visited me twice that summer, and in between we drew kinkiness out of each other in letters, long stories about naughty schoolgirls and perverted principals.

On my day off, at the Lee Jackson Motor Inn (named for not one but two Confederate generals), she presented me with a black slip from a thrift store and panties made of cheap rayon, still on the plastic hanger. I changed and lay on the bed on my stomach. When she told me to look at her she was sitting in an armchair, wearing a white button-down, open to show the weight of her breasts, black and silver scissors dangling from her fingers. The cold metal on my back was more welcome than any warm caress.

She sliced off the slip, and with it, my resistance, my insecurity. I was a long-anticipated gift, a hidden treasure. She called me filthy names and tied my hands to a hook in the closet with cotton clothesline. We were amateurs. We didn't know any better. We ripped the hook out of the wall.

She fucked the femme into me.

THE OUTSIDE EDGE

Sacchi Green

Suli was fire and wine, gold and scarlet, lighting up the dim passageway where we waited.

I leaned closer to adjust her Spanish tortoiseshell comb. A cascade of dark curls brushed my face, shooting sparks all the way down to my toes, but even a swift, tender kiss on her neck would be too risky. I might not be able to resist pressing hard enough to leave a dramatic visual effect the TV cameras couldn't miss.

Tenderness wasn't what she needed right now, and neither was passion. An edgy outlet for nervous energy would be more like it. "Skate a clean program," I murmured in her ear, "and maybe I'll let you get dirty tonight." My arm across her shoulders might have looked locker-room casual, but the look she shot me had nothing to do with team spirit.

"*Maybe*, Jude? You think maybe you'll *let* me?" She tossed her head. Smoldering eyes, made even brighter and larger by theatrical makeup, told me that I'd need to eat my words later before my mouth could move on to anything more appealing.

The other pairs were already warming up. Suli followed Tim into the arena, her short scarlet skirt flipping up oh-so-accidentally to reveal her firm, sweet ass. She wriggled, daring me to give it an encouraging slap, knowing all too well what the rear view of a scantily clad girl does for me.

I followed into the stadium and watched the action from just outside the barrier. As Suli and Tim moved onto the ice, the general uproar intensified. Their groupies had staked a claim near one end, and a small cadre of my own fans were camped out nearby, having figured out over the competition season that something was up between us. Either they'd done some discreet stalking, or relied on the same gaydar that had told them so much about me even before I'd fully understood it myself. Probably both.

Being gay wasn't, in itself, a career-buster these days. Sure, the rumormongers were eternally speculating about the men in their sequined outfits, but the skating community was united in a compact never to tell, and the media agreed tacitly never to ask. A rumor of girl-on-girl sex would probably do nothing more than inspire some fan fiction in certain blogging communities. That didn't mean there weren't still lines you couldn't cross in public, especially in performance—lines I was determined, with increasing urgency, to cross once and for all.

But I didn't want to bring Suli down if I fell. That discussion was something we kept avoiding, and whenever I tried to edge toward it she'd distract me in ways I couldn't resist.

Suli's the best, I thought now in the stadium, watching her practice faultless jumps with Tim. You'd never guess what she'd been doing last night with me, while the other skaters were preparing for the performance of their lives with more restful rituals. She'd already set records in pairs skating, and next year, at my urging, she was going to go solo. It was a good thing I wouldn't be competing against her.

I won't be competing against anybody, I thought, my mind wandering as the warm-up period dragged on.

It had taken me long enough to work it out, focusing on my skating for so many years, but the more I appreciated the female curves inside those scanty, seductive costumes, the less comfortable I was wearing them. Cute girls in skimpy outfits were just fine with me—bodies arched in laybacks, or racing backward, glutes tensed and pumping, filmy fabric fluttering in the breeze like flower petals waving to the hungry bees—but I'd rather see than be one.

I'd have quit mainstream competition if they hadn't changed the rules to allow long-legged "unitards" instead of dresses. That concession wasn't enough to make me feel really comfortable, though, and I knew my coach was right that some judges would hold it against me if I didn't wear a skirt at least once in a while. This year I'd alternated animal-striped unitards with a Scottish outfit just long enough to preserve the mystery of what a Scotsman wears under his kilt, assuming that he isn't doing much in the way of spins or jumps or spirals. I knew this for certain, having experimented in solitary practice with my own sturdy six inches of silicon pride.

So why not just switch to the Gay Games? Or follow Rudy Galindo and Surya Bonaly to guest appearances on SkateOut's Cabaret on Ice?

If you have a shot at the Olympics, the Olympics are where you go, that's why. Or so I'd thought. But I was only in fifth place after the short program—maybe one or two of the judges weren't that keen on bagpipe music—and a medal was too long a shot now.

I knew, deep down, what the problem was. Johanna, the coach we shared, had urged me to study Suli's style in hopes that some notion of elegance and grace might sink into my thick head. Suli had generously agreed to try to give me at least a trace of an artistic clue. But the closer we became, the more I'd rebelled against faking a feminine grace and elegance that were so naturally hers, and so unnatural for me.

This would be my last competition, no matter what. Maybe I'd get a pro gig with a major ice show, maybe I wouldn't. If I did, it would be on my own terms. "As God is my witness, I'll never be girlie again!" I'd proclaimed melodramatically to Suli last night.

"Works just fine for me," she'd said, kneeling with serene poise to take my experimental six inches between her glossy, carmined lips and deep into her velvet throat.

Ten minutes later, serenity long gone, I stood braced against the edge of the bed and bore her weight while she clamped her thighs around my hips and her cunt around my pride, locked her hands behind my neck, and rode me with fierce, pounding joy. I dug my fingers into her asscheeks to steady her, and to add to the driving force of her lunges. Small naked breasts slapped against mine on each forward stroke. When I could catch one succulent nipple in my mouth her cries would rise to a shriller pitch, but then she'd jerk roughly away to get more leverage for each thrust.

My body ached with strain and arousal and the friction of the harness. My mind was a blur of fantasies. *We're whirling in the arena, my skates carving spirals into the ice, her dark hair lifting in the wind...*

"Spin me!" Suli suddenly arched her upper body into a layback position, arms no longer gripping me but raised into a pleading curve. Adrenaline, muscles, willpower; none of it was enough now. Only speed could keep us balanced. I stepped back from the bed and spun in place, swinging her in one wide circle, then another, tension hammering through my clit hard enough to counter the burn of the leather gouging my flesh.

Suli's voice whipped around us, streaming as free as her hair. I held on, battling gravity, riding the waves of her cries, until, as they crested, the grip of her legs around me began to slip. In two lurching steps I had her above the bed again, and in another second she was on the sheets. I pressed on until her breathing began to slow, and then covered her tender breasts and mouth with a storm of kisses close to bites until I had to arch back and pump and grind my way to a noisy release of my own.

When we'd sprawled together in delirious exhaustion long enough for our panting to ease, I raised up to gaze at her. The world-famous princess of poise and grace lay tangled in her own wild hair, lips swollen, skin streaked with sweat, and most likely bruised in places where the TV cameras had better not reach.

"And *you* lectured *me* about never jumping without knowing exactly where I was going to land!" I said. "How did you know I wouldn't drop you?"

"Aren't you always bugging me to let you try lifts?" she countered drowsily. "You've spun me before, on the ice; you're tall and strong enough." She rolled over on top of me and murmured into the hollow of my throat, "Anyway, I did know where I was going to land. And I knew that you'd get me there. You always do." Then her head slumped onto my shoulder and her body slid down to nestle in the protective curve of mine. In seconds she was asleep.

I always will, I mouthed silently, but couldn't say it aloud. Giving way to tenderness, to emotions deeper than the pyrotechnics of sex, was more risk than I could handle. Wherever I was going to land, she belonged somewhere better. *How am I going to bear it? How can we still be together?*

* * *

I shook my head to clear it. Suli and Tim were gliding with the rest of the competitors toward the edge of the ice, and I realized suddenly that it was time to take my seat in the stands. The final grouping of the pairs long program was about to get underway.

Suli and Tim skated third, to music from Bizet's *Carmen*. Somebody always skates to *Carmen*, but no one ever played the part better than Suli. The dramatic theme of love and betrayal was a perfect setting for her, and today the passionate beat of the "Habanera" was a perfect match for my jealous mood.

Watching Tim with Suli on the ice always drove me crazy. When his hand slid from the small of her back to her hip I wanted to lunge and chew it off at the wrist. His boyfriend Thor, a speed skater with massively muscled thighs, would have been highly displeased by that, so it was just as well that I resisted the impulse.

It wasn't really the way Tim touched Suli that burned me. Well, okay, maybe it was, with every nuance of the traditional lifts and holds pulsing with erotic innuendo. Still, my hands knew her needs far better than he ever could, or cared to. But he was allowed to do it publicly, artistically, acting out scenarios of fiery love—and I wasn't. Knowing that the delectable asscheeks filling the taut scarlet seat of her costume bore bruises in the shapes of my fingers was only small comfort.

His other hand rested lightly on her waist as they whirled across the ice. Any second—in six more beats—she would jump, and with simultaneous precision he would lift, and throw... *Now!* For all the times I'd seen it, my breath still caught. Suli twisted impossibly high into the air, and far out...out...across the ice...

Yes! Throw triple axel! A perfect one-footed landing flowing into a smooth, graceful follow-through, and then up into a double loop side by side with Tim in clockwork synchronicity.

It was the best. The audience knew it, the judges knew it. I knew it, and admiration nearly won out over envy when Tim lifted Suli high overhead, her legs spread wide, in the ultimate hand-in-crotch position known as The Helicopter. Envy surged back. Her crotch would be damp with sweat and excitement, not the kind I could draw from her, but still! Then she dropped abruptly past his face, thighs briefly scissoring his neck, pussy nudging his chin. I shook, nearly whimpering, as Suli slid sensuously down along Tim's body. As soon as her blades touched down she leaned back, back, impossibly far back, until her hair brushed the ice in a death spiral. I tensed as though my hand, not Tim's, gripped hers to brace her just this side of disaster.

A few judges always took points off for "suggestive" material. What did they think pairs skating was all about, if not sex? But it was a technically clean and ambitious program, beautifully executed. Suli and Tim won the gold medals they deserved.

I got no chance to go for the gold of Suli's warm body that night. When I came up behind her in our room and reached around to cup her breasts, she wriggled her compact butt against me, and then turned and shoved me away.

"No," she decreed, putting a finger across my lips as I tried to speak. I nibbled at it instead. "You have your long program tomorrow, and I know better than you do what you need."

I tried to object, with no luck.

"Sure," Suli went on, "fast and furious sex and complete exhaustion were just what I needed, but you'll do better saving up that energy and channeling the tension into your skating."

"It doesn't matter," I said sulkily. "I can't medal now anyway. I was thinking, in fact, that this might as well be the time..."

She knew what I meant. "No!" Her scowl was at least as alluring as her smiles. "You can still win the bronze, if you want it enough. At least two of those prima donnas ahead of you have never skated a clean long program in their lives. Medal, and you get into the exhibition at the end. That's the time to make your grand statement to the world." She saw my hesitation, and gripped my shoulders so hard her nails dug in. "Think of Johanna! You can't disgrace your coach during actual competition. And think of your fans!" Her expression eased into a smile she couldn't suppress. Her grip eased. "Okay, your fans would love every minute of it. I've seen the signs they flip at you when they're sure the cameras can't see. 'We Want Jude, Preferably in the Nude!'" She drew her fingers lightly across my chest and downward. "Can't say that I blame them."

Suli was so close that her warm scent tantalized me. I thought I was going to get some after all, but the kiss I grabbed was broken off all too soon, leaving me aching for more.

"Please, Jude, do it this way." She stroked my face, brushing back my short dark hair. I wasn't sure I could bear her gentleness. "Even your planned routine comes close enough to the edge. One way or another, it will be worth it. I promise."

So I did it her way, and skated the long program I'd rehearsed so many times. Inside, though, I was doing it my way at last, and not much caring if it showed.

I skated to a medley from the Broadway show *Cats*. My black unitard with white down the front and at the cuffs was supposed to suggest a "tuxedo" cat with white paws. The music swept from mood to mood, poignance to nostalgia to swagger, but no matter what character a song was meant to suggest, in my mind and gut I was never, for a moment, anybody's sweet pussy. I was every inch a Tom. Tomcat prowling urban roofs and alleys; tomboy tumbling the dairymaid in the hay; top-hatted Tom in the back streets of Victorian London pinching the housemaids' cheeks, fore and aft.

Suli had been right about storing up tension and then letting it spill out. Like fantasy during sex, imagination sharpened my performance. Each move was linked to its own notes of the music, practiced often enough to be automatic, but tonight my footwork was more precise, my spins faster, my jumps higher and landings smoother. I had two quad jumps planned, something none of my rivals would attempt, and for the first time I went into each of them with utter confidence.

The audience, subdued at first, was with me before the end, clapping, stomping, whistling. I rode their cheers, pumped with adrenaline as though we were all racing toward some simultaneous climax, and in the last minute I turned a planned double-flip, double-toe-loop into a triple-triple, holding my landing on a back outer edge as steadily as though my legs were fresh and rested.

The crowd's roar surged as the music ended. Fans leaned above the barrier to toss stuffed animals, mostly cats, onto the ice, and one odd flutter caught my eye in time for a detour to scoop up the offering. Sure enough, the fabric around the plush kitten's neck was no ribbon, but a pair of lavender panties. Still warm. It wasn't the first time.

Suli waited at the gate. I gave her a cocky grin and thrust the toy into her hands. Her expressive eyebrows arched higher, and then she grinned back and swatted my butt with it.

The scoring seemed to take forever. "Half of them are scrambling to figure out if you've broken any actual rules," Johanna muttered, "and scheming to make up some new ones if you haven't." The rest, though, must have given me everything they had. The totals were high enough to get me the bronze medal, even when none of the following skaters quite fell down.

Suli stuck by me every minute except for the actual awards ceremony, and she was right at the front of the crowd then. In the cluster of fans following me out of the arena, a few distinctly catlike "Mrowrr's!" could be heard, and then good-humored laughter as Suli threw an arm around me and aimed a ferocious "Growrr!" back over her shoulder at them.

Medaling as a long shot had condemned me to a TV interview. The reporter kept her comments to the usual inanities, except for a somewhat suggestive, "That was quite some program!"

"If you liked that, don't miss the exhibition tomorrow," I said to her, and to whatever segment of the world watches these things. When I added that I was quitting competition to pursue my own "artistic goals," she flashed her white teeth and wished me luck, and then, microphone set aside and camera off, leaned close for a moment to lay a hand on my arm. "Nice costume, but I'll bet you'll be glad to get it off."

Suli was right on it, her own sharp teeth flashing and her long nails digging into my sleeve. The reporter snatched her hand back just in time. "Don't worry," Suli purred, "I've got all that covered."

Don't expose yourself like that! Don't let me drag you down! But I couldn't say it, and I knew Suli was in no mood to listen.

I was too tired, anyway, wanting nothing more than to strip off the unitard and never squirm into one again, but Suli wouldn't let me change in the locker room. Once I saw the gleam of metal she flashed in her open shoulder bag—so much for security at the Games!—I followed her out and back to our room with no regret for the parties we were missing.

The instant the door clicked shut behind us she had the knife all the way out of its leather sheath. "Take off that medal," she growled, doing a knockout job of sounding menacing. "The rest is mine."

I set the bronze medal on the bedside table, flopped backward onto the bed, and spread my arms and legs wide. "Use it or lose it," I said, and then gasped at the touch of the hilt against my throat.

"Don't move," she ordered, crouching over me, her hair brushing my chest. I lay frozen, not a muscle twitching, although my flesh shrank reflexively from the cold blade when she sat back on her haunches and slit the stretchy unitard at the juncture of thigh and crotch.

"Been sweating, haven't we," she crooned, slicing away until the fabric gaped like a hungry mouth, showing my skin pale beneath. "But it's not all sweat, is it?" Her cool hand slid inside to fondle my slippery folds. It certainly wasn't all sweat.

Her moves were a blend of ritual and raw sex. The steel flat against my inner thigh sent tongues of icy flame stabbing deep into my cunt. The keen edge drawn along my belly and breastbone seemed to split my old body and release a new one, though only a few light pricks drew blood. The rip of the fabric parting under Suli's knife and hands and, eventually, teeth, was like the rending of bonds that had confined me all my life.

Then Suli's warm mouth captured my clit. The trancelike ritual vanished abruptly in a fierce, urgent wave of right here, right now, right *NOW NOW NO-O-W-W-W-W!* Followed, with hardly a pause to recharge, by further waves impelled by her teasing tongue and penetrating fingers until I was completely out of breath and wrung out.

"I thought I was supposed to be storing up energy," I told her, when I could talk at all.

"Jude, you're pumping out enough pheromones to melt ice," Suli said, "and I'm not ice!"

It turned out that I wasn't all that wrung out after all, and if I couldn't talk, it was only because Suli was straddling my face, and my mouth was most gloriously, and busily, full.

The chill kiss of the blade lingered on my skin the next day, along with the heat of Suli's touch. I passed up the chance to do a run-through of my program, which didn't cause much comment since it was just the exhibition skate. Johanna, who knew what I was up to, took care of getting my music to the sound technicians with no questions asked.

There were plenty of questioning looks, though, when I went through warm-up muffled in sweats and a lightweight hoodie. Judging from the buzz among my fans, they may have been placing bets. Anybody who'd predicted the close-cropped hair with just enough forelock to push casually back, and the unseen binding beneath my plain white T-shirt, would have won. The tight blue jeans looked genuinely worn and faded, and from any distance the fact that the fabric could stretch enough for acrobatic movement wasn't obvious.

It was my turn at last. Off came the sweats and hoodie. I took to the ice, rocketing from shadows into brightness, and then stopped so abruptly that ice chips erupted around the toes of my skates. There were squeals, and confused murmurs; I was aware of Suli, still in costume from her own performance, watching from the front row.

Then my music took hold.

Six bars of introduction, a sequence of strides and glides—and I was Elvis, "Lookin' for Trouble," leaping high in a spread eagle, landing, and then twisting into a triple-flip, double-toe-loop. My body felt strong. And free. And *true*.

Then I was "All Shook Up," laying a trail of intricate footwork the whole length of the rink, tossing in enough cocky body-work to raise an uproar. Elvis Stojko or Philippe Candeloro couldn't have projected more studly appeal. When my hips swiveled—with no trace of a feminine sway—my fans went wild.

They subsided as the music slowed to a different beat, slower, menacing. "Mack the Knife" was back in town: challenge, swagger, jumps that ate up altitude, skate blades slicing the ice in sure, rock-steady landings. Then, in a final change of mood, came the aching, soaring passion of "Unchained Melody." I let heartbreak show through, loneliness, sorrow, desperate longing.

In my fantasy a slender, long-haired figure skated in the shadows just beyond my vision, mirroring my moves with equal passion and unsurpassable grace. Through the haunting strains of music I heard the indrawn breaths of a thousand spectators, and then a vast communal sigh. I was drawing them into my world, making them see what I imagined...I jumped, pushing off with all my new strength, spun a triple out into an almost effortless quad, landed—and saw what they had actually seen.

Suli glided toward me, arms outstretched, eyes wide and bright with challenge. I stopped so suddenly I would have fallen if my hands hadn't reached out reflexively to grasp hers. She moved backward, pulling me toward her, and then we were skating together as we had so often in our private predawn practice sessions. The music caught us, melded us into a pair. Suli moved away, rotated into an exquisite layback spin, slowed, stretched out her hand, and my hand was there to grasp hers and pull her into a close embrace. Her raised knee pressed up between my legs with a force she would never have exerted on Tim. I wasn't packing, but my clit lurched with such intensity that I imagined it bursting through my jeans.

Then we moved apart again, aching for the lost warmth, circling, now closer, now farther...the music would end so soon...Suli flashed a quick look of warning, mouthed silently, "Get ready!" and launched herself toward me.

Hands on my shoulders, she pushed off, leapt upward, and hung there for a moment while I gripped her hips and pressed my mouth into her belly. Then she wrapped her legs around my waist and arched back. We spun slowly, yearningly, no bed, this time, to take the weight of our hunger. And then, as the last few bars of music swelled around us, Suli slid sensuously down my body until she knelt in a pool of scarlet silk at my feet. She looked up into my eyes, and finally, gracefully and deliberately, bowed her head and rested it firmly against my crotch as the last notes faded away.

An instant of silence, of stillness, followed, until the crowd erupted in chaos, cheers and applause mingling with confusion and outrage. TV cameras were already converging on our exit. I pulled Suli up so that my mouth was close to her ear; her hair brushing my cheek still made me tingle.

"Suli, what have you done? What will—?"

She shushed me with a finger across my lips. "Sometimes, if you can't stand to be left behind, you *do* have to jump without knowing exactly where you'll land."

So I kissed her right there on the ice for the world to see. Then, hand in hand, we skated toward the gate to whatever lay beyond.

I'VE BEEN AROUND THE BLOCK, THREE TIMES, MAYBE FOUR

Danielle de Santiago

When did you first know you were Canadian?
—Dame Edna to k. d. lang

I'm always kind of surprised when other women tell me about their coming out and how they figured out that they are lesbians. They tell me about subtle and slow developments; about secret looks they gave their female friends, about bad and unsatisfying relationships they had with men, and how they finally, slowly, step by step, discovered that they liked women. With me it was totally different; it didn't come quietly, on velvet kitten feet. No, with me it was something sudden. One day it was just there. It was like waking up.

When I was a teenager in Westphalia, Germany, I dated boys of my own age. It wasn't bad. They treated me well, and I never felt displeased. I never felt unsatisfied—but I also didn't fall in love. I never felt this excitement, this wild and stormy feeling of lust my girlfriends told me about. I never sat by the soccer field and gossiped with the other girls about how well my boyfriend could kiss, about how strong his arms were and how firm his butt was. No.

To be honest, I didn't even realize that my boyfriend had a butt! He was certainly the guy I considered to be my boyfriend, but still he was just a good friend. We only met on weekends, a rule of my parents that was very suitable for me. A bit of kissing and making out didn't make me feel too uncomfortable. Aside from that, we just watched many, many movies in the theater, and he lent me a lot of his records...but no heart beating, no butterflies.

It went on like this with the next guy and the next. We got along very well, but I didn't fall in love, and it would be a while until I found out why it was like that.

One morning at the Free University Berlin, as I stood in the bathroom of the dorm and brushed my teeth, a girl from my French class told me that she had just learned that her boyfriend was cheating on her.

That girl's name was Michelle. She had long, shiny red hair I envied, and unbelievably big eyes that always seem to invite one to take a dip in them. She was one of the prettiest girls at the university, and while she told me about her cheating boyfriend I happened to think, *What an idiot! If I could be with such a wonderful girl, I would never cheat on her.*

If I could be with such a...girl?

There it was. *Lesbian* in big neon letters. All of a sudden it was crystal clear; I was a lesbian. But what now? Unfortunately life isn't an episode of "Ellen" where the unbelievably attractive Melissa Etheridge comes along with a piece of paper and welcomes you into the L-World after you have signed your coming-out papers.

The discovery that I was a lesbian didn't make things easier for me. No shit, Sherlock. Unluckily, no one tells you how you become a "real" lesbian. Inconspicuously I started to observe two girls, seniors, who were gossiped about as possible lesbians.

One of them, Joanne, was a discreet young woman with thick glasses and a tendency to wear men's pants. She was quiet and somewhat mysterious, a combination of bookworm and Victorian maiden. I was about to tell her that I was a lesbian, too, when I saw her one afternoon at the bus stop...holding hands with a guy who wore the same thick glasses as she did, and the same wide corduroy pants as well. Joanne wasn't a lesbian; she was just a nerd.

The other one, Melanie, was a totally different type of girl. She had shaved off her hair on the sides while the rest was piled up in a jet black crow's nest above her white-powdered face. Her lips and nails were also painted black, and sometime she smelled a bit strange. Was that what being lesbian was about? Was that the deal? Did I have to wear ripped-up fishnet stockings? Did I have to become a goth to be a lesbian?

I searched in the university library for help. Wasn't there some kind of advisor? Or lesbian books? No, at least not in the library. So I went to town. Berlin is a big city, much bigger than the little village in North Rhine-Westphalia where I grew up. Luckily, there were a couple of women's bookstores in Berlin Mitte and Prenzlauerberg.

There was a lot of literature, coffee table books, feminist books, computer books, poetry collections and—goddesses have mercy—lesbian books as well. At first I wasn't brave enough to pick up one of "those" books. Instead I sneaked for hours around the racks, flipped through cookbooks, and bought incense. How I would have loved to pick up one of these books! Instead I looked around with a feeling of shame. My gaze glided over the covers, until at last my fingertips followed. Here I saw everything the lesbian heart desires: *Best Lesbian Romance*; *Hot Lesbian Erotica*; *Rode Hard, Put Away Wet;* as well as *Susie Sexpert´s Lesbian Sexworld*. Finally, I held my breath and bought two books.

Later I sat in the park to read. I turned page after page and couldn't stop being amazed. I read about infatuating dykes on motorbikes, and vibrator parties and young lesbians in New York. How could it be that I was the only lesbian in my university while there were nightclubs full of them in other cities? Okay, I was far from being a club kid, but there had to be other ways to meet women. What should I do?

It couldn't be so hard to meet other lesbians. What else did I know about lesbians besides that they wore gothic makeup and rode motorcycles? Who were lesbians? And how could I become a real one? Were there rules? Orders? Secret passwords? Who were the best-known lesbians? Jodie? Ellen? Melissa? Suddenly I knew. Martina Navratilova! Sure, she was the most popular lesbian. So I borrowed a racket and pleaded with my sister to join me to play tennis. For four weeks she hunted me up and down the tennis court on each Saturday and played, unfortunately, a lot better than I did. And the lesbians? Well…there were no lesbians as far as I could see.

Finally I gave in to the nightclub possibility. If that was the only way to meet women, I would put on my dancing shoes. I read that a gay nightclub nearby had a lesbian night once a month, and that sounded like a good start, more like having a nice swim than jumping into the cold water. For weeks and weeks I prepared myself for the event, bought a new dress, high heels, and even thought about buying some black lipstick and matching nail polish, just in case.

Then the evening came. It was almost midnight when I made my entrance into the Joko. But what can I say? I had imagined it differently. Dizzy twilight lit up the club and the five or six women who stood at the bar, looking bored. Here I was, the only lesbian in a dress and with a purse. All the others wore rough boots and plaid shirts matching their LSHC (lesbian short haircuts) and looked with suspicion at me.

Everything will be all right. I tried to calm myself down. I told the girl behind the bar that I wanted to drink something. What? Of course what all the others drink too, I said. Though I would rather have had some Irish cream, the bartender served me a beer. Insecure, I smiled at the woman next to me who had a big Molly tattoo on her bicep, but she didn't react.

"Are you often here?" I tried to make some conversation.

"Yes, once a month," the woman answered. Not a very chatty fellow.

"I'm here for the first time today, and..." Before I could say any more the woman turned away from me. Why didn't she want to talk to me? "I have a tattoo as well," I wanted to shout at her. "I'm one of you! Don't you see that?" But...was that true? Was I really one of them? I didn't even own a lumberjack shirt. The only thing we had in common was that we were into women.

Maybe that was the problem. I wanted women who looked like women. I wanted long, silky hair, dresses of thin fabrics, and lips of sensual red. I wanted to kiss a girl who smelled like Jil Sander Sun perfume, wanted to touch and peel off her lingerie before we made love. I didn't have anything against the women in this bar, I didn't mind that they were butch, but that wasn't what I was looking for. I desired a femme.

Two weeks after the Joko fiasco I visited the women's bookstore again. By then I had been there more often and had become friends with Bettina, the owner. She wasn't a lesbian, but she always had a willing ear for my problems and tried to help me as far as possible. Usually Bettina offered me a cup of herbal tea, but this time she had something much better for me; the number of a new lesbian group.

"Why don't you just give them a call?" Bettina handed me a little lavender piece of paper with a picture of a violet next to the number.

Bettina was right. Why not just try? Wouldn't hurt. Would it? Still, I was unbelievably nervous. Finally I dialed the number, and a woman named Rita invited me to the next meeting of the group. Now that the date was fixed I was really, really scared. Every night I dreamed about a huge room with a huge table and many women who looked at me distrustfully, trying to find out if I were a lesbian for real.

At last the day came. It took me a while to find the right address, so I was a bit late when I finally arrived. My heart beat like crazy when I knocked on the door and a voice told me to come in. There wasn't a big table, and it seemed that I wasn't the only one who was late, since there were only three women in the room, sitting on an old couch. They were friendly and offered me a seat.

I had found them. The lesbians. All three of them. Because there weren't any more lesbians in this group.

Vera, Jeanette, and Rita. Three awesome and really nice middle-aged women who finally answered all my questions. Unfortunately, they too weren't what I had been looking for. I wanted to have fun, to enjoy life with women of my own age, and, finally, to fall in love. With these three women of my mom's age I felt rather like a novice who eagerly listened to her teachers. It was like visiting my aunts every two weeks to have coffee and cake while we talked about boys, or rather, girls.

But I stuck to my new group. I went to the meetings and the discussion groups, went with them to see plays at the city hall, and visited street fairs. After five months, two of the women moved away or started a new job, so I became the new group leader. Instead of the discussion groups we had billiard evenings, went to lunar parks, took road trips and bicycle tours, and started a bimonthly lesbian disco in the basement of the house.

What can I say? Suddenly they came, all kinds of lesbians: blondes and brunettes, with short and with long hair, ugly ones and beauties, smart ones and funny ones. Exciting women, boring and shy women. Students, dykes on bikes, doctors and single parents, teachers and chefs, artists and gym class teachers, butches and femmes...and among all these women, me. But not only me. She came, too. The one. The one I had waited for so long. Lina.

She wasn't exactly how I had imagined her. At the age of thirty-seven she was a bit older than I, and instead of dresses she wore soft black leather pants that fit perfectly around her long legs. Instead of blouses and tops she wore T-shirts from local rock bands with the sleeves cut off and men's undershirts, and her dark red hair was rather short. But she wore boots with high heels, owned a collection of lipsticks in seven different shades of red, and underneath her leather outfits (as I would eventually find out) she wore satin underwear.

It was desire at first sight, but still it took a while until shy flirting and secret looks became more. It happened on a warm summer evening. The group had spent the day at the Wannsee outside of Berlin where we chilled bottles of wine in the lake and grilled steaks and vegetables beside the shore. When the night came, all the women were sitting around the campfire, drinking wine and roasting sticky-sweet chocolate bananas.

All of a sudden there was a thunderous sound, and colorful lightning illuminated the sky. Rita yelled loudly, and two or three of the other women jumped up from their blankets, but it was just the yearly fireworks at the Peacocks' Isle fest on the other side of the lake. Its blossoms bloomed red, orange, and yellow and cast a mysterious light on the deep-hanging clouds.

Lina, who was sitting next to me, gave me a smile and stood up. "I'm going for a walk. Does someone want to join me?" All the other women giggled since Lina was looking directly at me.

"Well...sure," I said hastily, and rose with blushing cheeks to leave the fire with Lina. We walked along the waterfront and watched the last red and yellow sparks die above us. Suddenly I felt a touch at my hand, tender and silent, like a bird's heart. Lina's hand glided into mine.

"Don't walk so fast," she said, and stopped so that I had to stop walking too.

"What's up?" I asked nervously, and tried to see the fire far behind us.

"You know what's up. Don't you?" Lina laughed silently and came closer. "Look at me," she said. "I won't bite you. Well... maybe I will." Her hand came out of the dark and brushed the damp hair off of my forehead.

I tried to say something, but there were no words inside me. Instead, I finally felt the beating heart I had missed for so many years. I had craved it for such a long time, and now that it was here I felt like it was tearing my chest apart with...love? Was that love? It had to be.

I really didn't know what to say. Lina's eyes were so wonderful, expectant and green in the twilight. I just gave her a kiss. I needed all my strength to lift myself on my tiptoes, bring my face close to hers, and put my dry lips on her warm and soft mouth. Bang.

This must have been love, because what else could it be if this little touch took away all my fears? All of a sudden I felt like I could do everything. There was no *No* and no *When* and no *But.* I didn't know if what I was doing was right, but I knew I had to do it or die. Thoughts raced through my head while all kinds of sexual images lit up my mind. I was driven by every fantasy I had had about Lina during the last weeks, and she seemed to feel the same because her lips kissed me back right before she took a look around and then led me away from the water over to where the forest began.

"Lie down here," she whispered, and pushed me gently down on a soft bed of moss and grass growing under the oak trees beside the lake. Slowly, appreciatively, her shadow glided over me. Her fingers followed her shadow; they caressed me and pulled off my baggy T-shirt so I was left in only my bikini.

Lina smelled so good! Like real life, like Jil Sander Sun perfume, like tobacco and summer, like sex and like woman. Carefully she slid her arm under my neck and pulled me closer so I could feel her firm, muscular body underneath the cut-off army shorts and white tank top.

"That feels so good," she whispered into my hair and kissed me again, on my lips, my chin, my neck, and my boobs. Raw like a cat's tongue, hers wandered over my collarbone, down between my boobs, around my navel and lingered right above the edge of my bikini bottom until I couldn't stand it any longer and begged her to go on.

Giggling, she hooked her thumbs under my bikini and pulled it down over my legs. Then she lifted herself up and took off her shirt so I could see her small boobs and her white skin. Her feet touched me briefly when she took off her shorts and came back down beside me again.

For a moment I thought about who would do what and then decided to let Lina give directions. "Mmm," I moaned when her fingers started to slide across my legs and she kissed my knees.

"Everything all right?" she asked.

"Yes, everything is great. It just...feels so good," I answered.

"I haven't done that much yet," Lina whispered, her lips close to my ear again. That was true. She hadn't done so much yet, but still my cunt was wet and my nipples stiffened as I felt Lina's hot breath, like the dragon lady's exhalation in the fairy tale, burning my skin.

With a skilled movement she reached underneath me and unhooked my bikini top so that my breasts fell loose into the warm air. Greedily she clamped her mouth over one, then the other hard nipple. "Maybe we shouldn't do it here," I whispered weakly, half-hoping Lina wouldn't hear me at all.

"Why not?" she asked with a mouth full of nipple and breast.

"Well...just because of...the others," I sighed.

"I don't see any others," answered Lina, and I closed my eyes when she laid her hands on my knees and spread my legs carefully apart. Her hand was warm on me when she squeezed my damp crotch in a way I almost couldn't take.

She glided deeper between my thighs, explored me, and pushed my legs farther apart. "Like a butterfly," she said, and dipped first one, then two fingers into my wetness.

Moaning, I arched my back, pushed my hips toward Lina's fingers, and lifted myself up to come down on her hands while her thumb pressed hard against my clit. Again and again I pushed down on her fingers, rode them until I thought I wouldn't be able to keep myself from coming...and that was when Lina pulled her hand away from me.

"No, please, no," I moaned, and then opened my eyes when I felt Lina's hair on the insides of my thighs. Rough like the fur of a wolf it rubbed across my skin, leaving sparks that disappeared when Lina closed her mouth over my cunt. Hot and moist, her tongue slithered across my swollen clit, licked and sucked me while her fingers spread me open as wide as possible.

I closed my eyes and dug my fingers into her hair while she entered me again and again with her warm angel's tongue and made me moan like a little soft animal, an animal captured in a trap. I placed my legs over her strong shoulders and pulled her face deeper and deeper in my pulsing crotch.

Once more she pierced me with a finger, pushed it deeper, searching and demanding. An electric shock seemed to flash through me.

The sensation that her drilling tongue and her probing, turning finger caused inside me was almost violent in its intensity. It wasn't the kind of feeling I knew from touching myself. It didn't build up slowly; no, it was there within a second. Like a motorcycle that starts running all of a sudden it went through my center where Lina's finger drove me, down to the depths of my body where suddenly another kind of fireworks illuminated my inner night. It was so strong that it was nearly unbearable.

Lina had kidnapped me and brought me into this no-man's-land between ecstasy and lustful pain. I almost wished it would stop, while another part of me hoped this would go on forever. I pushed so hard against her finger that it nearly took my breath away when her broad hand smashed against my clit again. I tried to lift myself up on my elbows, but I couldn't find a hold on the mossy ground and I fell backward.

Suddenly I didn't want to escape anymore. Every resistance disappeared. What I felt now was like a breach in a dike, as if a part of me would be stretched out infinitely. My juices flowed and dripped off of Lina's hands and lips when something broke inside me, spilled out of me, and took me away with it into the night. Silently I screamed out, and somewhere out on the lake a bird answered my call and disappeared again, leaving me shivering under Lina's hands.

Grinning, she crept up to me, lay down next to my exhausted body, and shoved me gently onto my side so that I could feel her wet chest against my back and her hot face lying moist in the curve of my shoulders. "You know what?" I asked her with my eyes closed.

"Hm?" Lina murmured into my curls.

"I am...I am a lesbian," I said, knowing I finally had arrived where I belonged.

"A lesbian? Indeed?" Lina answered, pretending to be surprised

"Yes, and what a lesbian I am," I said. "You want me to prove it?"

WELLINGTON NIGHTS

Fran Walker

I just want to be friends are the six suckiest words in the English language. Annie said it after we'd been hanging out together for a month. I tried initiating a snog, and she stood up and gave me the "just friends" line. She and her ex-girlfriend, I found out the next day, had made up, and the ex was moving back from Auckland. I think Annie just used me to make her ex jealous.

Kerin said it after we'd kissed at the movies, made out on a park bench at the waterfront, and groped each other through our clothes in her car. No explanation from Kerin, just that lame "friends" crap, like somehow it would make up for dumping me. Or maybe she thought it sounded better than saying, "Sorry, your thighs are too fat for my tastes."

And Jane, hell, Jane hadn't even bothered to want to be friends. She showed up an hour and a half late for our first date, with some skinny blonde sitting in the passenger seat tooting the car horn and flouncing her long hair while Jane came to the door of my flat and canceled our date with more haste than civility.

The only girl I did just want to be friends with was my flatmate, Margaret. Margaret and I were both femmes, both cashiers at the New World grocery store in Upper Hutt, both nineteen, both looking for a nice butch. And, sadly, both virgins. At least I was, and I believed Margaret when she grumbled that she was, too.

I was still a virgin femme looking for a nice butch when the phone rang on a Wednesday evening in March. It was Margaret. She sounded half-sloshed. "Girlfriend, you have totally got to come down to the Duke. The place has gone wild."

"The Duke?" The gay-friendly dive in downtown Wellington had neither music nor billiards and barely filled half its bar stools even on a Friday night. We'd only been there a few times. "What's so wild?"

"Some kind of convention. Not sure what, exactly, but the place is full of granny dykes, and they're buying drinks like there's no tomorrow."

Free drinks? Hell, yes, I was on my way. I put on a clean scoop-necked T-shirt and the tight black jeans that sort of hid my fat thighs, jogged to the Upper Hutt station and just managed to catch the last Number 91, and then hopped off the bus after Lambton Quay. Walking down Cuba Street, I could hear the roar of voices twenty meters from the door of the Duke.

I wriggled through the doorway. Women—short, tall, thin, fat, young, old—packed the place. Mostly old, I realized, peering through the dingy gloom. Margaret had been right. The place was full of granny dykes. One gray-haired woman winked at me. Another beckoned me to her table, pointing to an empty stool. I smiled, shook my head, and struggled through the crowd. Where was Margaret?

I found my friend at the bar, grinning like an idiot, with a fuzzy navel in each hand. Four older women with rainbow bandanas hovered over her.

"Yo, girlfriend!" Margaret shrieked. "Ladies, this is...yo, girlfriend!"

I wondered just how many drinks she'd had. "Hi. I'm Alison."

After a chorus of "Hi, Alison's!", one woman asked me what I'd like to drink. No leers. No come-on winks or surreptitious pats on the shoulder. Just delighted smiles from a happy group of women who seemed happy to have me join them. Still, I felt uncomfortable, as if I were there under false pretences. I wasn't pretty. The difference in our ages wasn't reason enough for them to pay for my drinks.

"Erm, a glass of wine, please."

"Live it up, Ali! Have a sex on the beach," Margaret said, sloshing one of her fuzzy navels across my wrist. "They're your favorite."

"Order anything you like, honey. We're celebrating," one of the older women said.

"Just wine would be great. Margaret and I both have to be to work at eight tomorrow morning." I nudged my friend meaningfully.

"Screw work!" Margaret downed the rest of her drinks and sat both glasses on the bar with a bang. "It's party time!"

The women whooped, and two of them began dancing together to nonexistent music. Margaret grabbed their rainbow bandanas and waved them around like a cheerleader's pompoms.

"White wine or red?" the bartender asked.

Nearby, a tall woman with a salt-and-pepper ponytail caught my eye. She turned toward me, and one silver earring swayed against her shoulder: an ankh, the Egyptian symbol of life. The laugh lines around her eyes deepened when she smiled at me. She beckoned to the bartender. A few minutes later, the bartender handed me a slender glass of fizzing wine.

"From Natasha," the bartender said, nodding her head

toward the tall woman. "She says it's guaranteed to make you smile, and it won't give you a hangover."

Margaret was shouting out her life story to her rainbow foursome. I eased back from the bar and took a sip of the champagne. The bubbles frothed over my teeth, tickled my tongue, and danced down my throat like some kind of magical fairy dust. I found myself smiling.

"Hi. I'm Natasha."

I looked up. Her laugh lines crinkled again as she grinned. How old was she—forty? Forty-five? Her eyebrows and eyelashes were still thick and dark, though her hair was mostly silver. A solid, stocky body, like a construction worker's. She raised her own glass of champagne and touched it to mine. The noisy crowd drowned out the clink.

"I'm Alison. Thanks for this." I indicated the champagne. "It's really nice."

"My pleasure." She sipped her champagne, holding her glass with one square hand. I looked closer: blunt, strong fingers; short nails—butch hands. Something inside me quivered.

I followed her to a table in the corner. Over three glasses of champagne, she explained to me who the celebrating women were: forty-odd lesbians from all over New Zealand whose poetry in a book called *Tapestry* had won some big literary prize. I nodded a lot and missed half of what she said; the noise level in the Duke got louder and louder, and my attention kept wandering to her hands. Those strong, square hands.

It was nearly eleven o'clock when I went to pee, and I found myself behind Margaret in the queue for the toilets. She was still listing to one side but seemed to be sobering up.

"Let's get a taxi home," Margaret said.

"Are you leaving now?"

"Yeah." She lowered her voice. "We need to get out before the grannies ask to get paid for the drinks."

I frowned. "I don't think they're expecting anything in return. They're just being nice."

"Better safe than sorry," Margaret muttered in my ear. "Let's nip out the back so we don't have to kiss any prune lips good-bye."

"I'm going to stay a while longer."

Margaret shrugged and disappeared into a toilet cubicle. By the time I'd peed and washed my hands, she was gone. I returned to Natasha's table.

"What was your poem in the book about?" I asked.

Natasha ran an idle finger around the rim of her champagne glass. "About teaching. How the old teach the young, and how the old learn as much from the teaching as the young do." Her finger circled the glass. I wondered what it would feel like to have that strong, blunt finger touching me, circling my nipples, circling my clitoris...I squeezed my knees together.

"Are you a teacher?" My voice sounded hoarse.

"Not a schoolteacher. But I do teach. I run a creative writing class, and I also teach life skills at a homeless shelter."

What would it be like to have the surety and confidence to teach, to work with homeless people, to write poetry? Maybe it was something that came with age, like gray hair and wrinkles. But Natasha didn't seem like anyone's nana. Her mouth didn't look like a prune. Her lips looked strong and purposeful, like her hands. I watched her single earring twirl and catch the light.

"I'll fetch us another drink." Natasha placed her hands flat on the table and pushed back her stool. I didn't feel the least bit tipsy, but the champagne was fizzing between my thighs. As she stood up, I reached out and touched my fingertip to hers.

She stopped, looked directly at me, and then circled my fingertip with her own.

I twined my index finger around hers. She slid her fingertip along my finger, up and down, and then around and up my thumb.

I was glad I hadn't left with Margaret.

My knees trembled. A shudder ran up my arm and down my spine. After an endless moment, I noticed some women at the next table watching us. Heat flooded my cheeks.

Natasha flicked a look at the next table and then turned back to me and withdrew her hand. "What would you be comfortable with?"

"Somewhere...somewhere more private," I managed to say.

She took my hand. We walked out of the Duke and into the cool night air.

"I have a hotel room just up the street," Natasha said.

I nodded. We walked in silence. My fingers felt hot twined with hers. I took short, fast breaths. We walked past reception, rode up the lift, and entered Natasha's room without my even noticing which hotel we'd entered.

"It's okay to just sit here and continue our conversation, if you like," Natasha said, switching on a lamp near the bed. "We don't have to—"

I must have gaped at her like an idiot. She smiled, moved closer, and bent her head. Her lips touched mine. Her strong hand settled at my waist.

My knees buckled. She caught me as I sagged.

She laughed softly. "Whoa there, tiger!"

I clung to her, clamped my hand over hers to hold it against my waist, and pulled her mouth down to mine. She kissed me again and then straightened.

"I'm old enough to be your mother, Alison."

"I don't want a mother. I want a teacher. Teach me."

"Have you never...?"

I shook my head. Slowly, I touched her cheek, her neck, and

then stroked her ponytail. I ran my fingers down her bare arm to her hand. Oh, god, those strong hands. "You're beautiful."

She pulled me over to the bed. My mouth met hers as she unfastened my jeans and pushed them over my hips, and then pulled my shirt up. We broke long enough for her to yank my shirt over my head. I lay down in my bra and panties. She shucked off her clothes and climbed over me, naked. Her hands stroked my body.

"You're beautiful," she breathed.

I felt beautiful under her gaze. My too-big bottom and thighs, my long nose, my stubby eyelashes—they all became beautiful as she kissed me, licked my throat, sucked at my bottom lip. I shivered. The tremors slithered down my body and centered between my legs. I smelled my own desire.

Natasha removed my bra and panties without my even realizing it. She cupped my bare breasts, and then squeezed. Hard, strong, firm, blunt hands, just as I'd imagined. My nipples stiffened against her palms. My breath came out in a long, quivering sigh.

"If there's anything you want..." Natasha said.

"You. I want you." Every sexual act and technique I'd fantasized about in my lonely bed, or read in books, or seen in movies left me in a rush, leaving behind nothing but blind, pulsating desire. I had no idea what I wanted her to do, but I wanted her to do it. Now.

She lapped at my nipple. Her hand slid down my belly. Lower. Lower.

My knees fell apart. My thighs trembled. Her fingers stroked me, and I felt how slickly wet I'd become.

She slid one finger inside me, then two, then three. I pushed down, wanting more. She thrust her fingers in and out, sucking on my nipple with a matching rhythm.

My breath caught. She moved her hand faster. Her thumb bumped my clitoris. I gasped and twisted to increase the pressure. She thrust her fingers in me harder and harder, rubbing her thumb against my clitoris with each stroke.

Her teeth scraped my nipple. I surged up against her hand and cried out. My legs went rigid and my hands clenched. My whole body spasmed. She rocked her hand against me, pressing rather than stroking my clitoris, as I shuddered and panted.

Ages later, I leaned up on one elbow.

"Wow."

Natasha tossed her ponytail back and grinned. "There was a fair bit of wow in that for me, too."

I reached out and touched her heavy breasts tipped with brown nipples. She turned to give me easier access. More confident now, I explored with my fingertips, my eyes, my tongue. I became fascinated by the ridges and puckers of each nipple, the change in her skin's texture where nipple turned to breast, the flesh that was both yielding and solid.

She captured one of my hands and tugged it to her leg. "Touch me."

I slid my hand up her thigh and then down the other. In between, her wetness coated my fingers. I touched her there again. Silky, pillow soft, and so slippery that there seemed to be no contours at all.

She moaned. Amazingly, she was as aroused as I had been. Her musky scent filled my nostrils.

A warm glow washed over me. I felt powerful. Beautiful.

I slid my fingers forward and then back. My fingertip slipped inside her as if pulled in by her desire. She pressed herself against me. I mimicked her earlier movements: sliding in first one finger, then two, then three. I raised my thumb. Her clitoris felt swollen, hot. She moaned again as I rubbed it.

She rolled on top of me. My hand slid out of her. Breast to breast, belly to belly, groin to groin, we rubbed together. I parted my legs, and she pressed herself closer to me. Her coarse curls rubbed my clitoris. Then her clitoris pressed mine, rubbing, grinding. I panted and wrapped my arms and legs around her and moved with her, following the pleasure, a sensual joy that I wanted to go on forever.

She made a series of small sounds, animal-like, as she pounded faster and faster against me. I caught her breast in my hand, raised my head, and drew her nipple into my mouth. She gasped, never slowing her movements. I licked her nipple and then grazed my teeth along it as I sucked it in and out of my mouth.

Natasha cried out, high and sharp, and slumped atop me.

Wrapped around each other, we slept. Twice in the night we woke. The first time we kissed and caressed and talked about our childhoods; the second time her caresses became more purposeful, and once again I exploded with pleasure. At seven in the morning, Natasha kissed me good-bye. She wouldn't give me her phone number or email address. We were from different generations, she said, different worlds. One night had been enough. She had taught me what I needed to know.

My heart knew she was right. We couldn't even be just friends. But my body didn't want to say good-bye.

"Where do you want to go tonight?" Margaret asked. "Tatou, the Blue Room, the Pound? It's drag night at the Pound. Or the women's rugby team will be at Blend's tonight. Or we could go to M & S—Eteta said she and Lynne will be there, it's karaoke night."

Margaret had stopped teasing me about my older woman fetish, and seemed intent instead on "curing" me by dragging me on pub crawls every other night. But I was sick of the Courtney

Place bars, the rave and techno music, the drunk students puking on the footpaths. I was sick of hiding at a corner table trying to look dykey enough that no guys would bother me, but not so dykey that I looked butch instead of femme; of worrying that a woman would walk up to me and then visibly decide not to ask me to dance because she didn't like my long nose and stubby eyelashes. Or, worse, that she would ask me to dance and then I'd have to stand up and she'd see my fat thighs.

"Nah, I'm going to stay home tonight," I lied.

"No worries," Margaret said cheerfully. "I'll join Eteta and Lynne."

After Margaret went out, I took a shower. I knew damned well where I was going tonight. I'd managed to stay away from the Duke for three months, after sitting there every night for nearly two weeks hoping against hope to see Natasha again. Tonight, though, I'd go back. Not for Natasha. But to remember. Just to remember what it was like to talk to someone about art and poetry and politics and feminism, someone who was smart and funny and kind, someone who made me feel interesting and beautiful and confident.

The Duke was as dingy as usual and smelled of stale beer. They'd installed a tinny radio behind the bar, and it was playing some godawful country western twangy music. I sat at the table Natasha and I had shared, drank a Speight's Dark, and cringed at the sound of a nasal-voiced man whinging about his achy breaky heart.

I wasn't heartbroken. I hadn't been in love with Natasha. I liked her and admired her and was grateful to her, but I knew that I didn't want her to come back. What I wanted back was the feeling I'd had that night with her, the person I'd become with her.

A woman walked up to the bar and spoke with the bartender,

who nodded and changed the radio station. I rained silent blessings on her head and tapped my foot in time to the Mint Chicks tune.

Some girls about my age, all with perfect faces and expensive-looking nose rings and slender hips hugged by low-cut jeans, got up and started dancing in a circle.

The woman went back to her table. I'd never seen her before. Lean, almost skinny, in baggy trousers, probably in her mid-twenties, with pale crew-cut hair. But the way she walked, the set of her shoulders—she had Natasha's confidence.

And she was looking at me. Smiling.

She stood up.

I stood up.

She walked over to my table. "Hi. I'm Ruth. Want to dance?"

My nose wasn't too long. My legs weren't too fat. Ruth had a look on her face that said I was just right. We moved next to the nose-ring girls and kind of swayed back and forth a bit. Ruth was still smiling.

She put her hands on my hips and pulled me a little closer. Her hair was white, not just pale. It didn't look frosted; prematurely gray, I guessed. It made a fascinating contrast with her face: old hair, young body.

Her crew cut looked soft and stiff at the same time. I wanted to rub my hand over it. Shyly, I put my hand on her forearm instead: smooth, silky skin, hard muscle beneath.

I leaned even closer. My hips touched hers. Something hard bumped the seam of my jeans. I tried to look down without looking as if I were looking down, but her gaze followed mine. Our foreheads touched. We stood there, staring at our crotches. And now I saw the bulge beneath her loose trousers.

My whole body went stiff. I couldn't swallow, thinking of her clitoris rubbing mine and feeling a rigid hardness in me at the same time. The blood roared in my ears.

"Does it bother you?" Ruth asked.

I opened my mouth. Nothing came out. All I could do was suck in air.

Ruth took a step back. Her head lowered, and she began to turn away.

I grabbed her hips, and pulled her to me.

"I do not want to just be friends," I said firmly.

She smiled and curled an arm around my shoulder.

"Me neither," Ruth said.

We danced, closer, faster. Small, soft breasts pressed against my chest. Hard desire pressed against my crotch.

I hoped I'd be learning something new tonight.

Remembering how a soft bite on my nipple had tipped me over the edge when I'd neared orgasm, and how the same move had brought Natasha to her climax, I smiled. Ruth might learn something new tonight, too.

GIRLS AND THEIR CARS

Renée Strider

It started out as a joke—until things got a little out of control.

Carole and Janis each owned a Lexus. They were extremely proud of their cars and kept them in tip-top shape, always clean and shiny, motors purring, every bell and whistle working.

Carole was into old luxury cars. Her previous car had been a twenty-year-old Caddy. Her Lexus, which she'd had for about four years, was a shimmering, silver gray sedan. A very big sedan, one of the first from the early '90s, with a very big V-8 engine.

Janis preferred newer, more sporty cars. She was driving a Porsche when she decided she needed something "more practical." So, about a year ago, she'd bought an almost-new, gleaming black Lexus. A high-performance SUV that looked a little dangerous, at least in comparison with Carole's—let's face it—more sedate car.

Did Janis get her Lexus as a *nyah, nyah* to Carole? Their friends wondered. The two certainly competed in other areas and had done so from almost the day—well, night, at the lesbian bar—that Janis moved into town a couple of years back. Moved into Carole's territory, really, because Carole was the number one player in town and suddenly had to make room for another dyke who went after the ladies—the femmes—with just as much charm and enthusiasm, and with just as much success.

On the surface, the competition between the two was friendly, whether it was over women, pool, or cars. At the bar they would often discuss cars, especially their "Lexi," offering advice to each other and comparing specs till their friends would roll their eyes from boredom. But sometimes there was an edge to it—a sarcastic comment from Janis, a pointed joke from Carole—and those around them would widen their eyes or smirk knowingly.

That's how it went one midsummer Saturday night at Red Emma's. The whole crowd was there, including most of our heroes' past conquests. Nobody was completely sober, but nobody was really drunk, either. Both Carole and Janis were between girlfriends. That happened a lot—though not necessarily at the same time—a reluctance to commit being the *sine qua non* of playerhood.

It was close to midnight, and Carole was standing comfortably with her back against the bar, one knee bent, boot heel hooked over the brass rail near the floor. Her pelvis was tilted forward both for balance and for effect. In her right hand she hefted a bottle of beer, while the thumb of the other hand stuck through a belt loop of her black jeans. She turned her head slightly and nodded as Abby, her companion at the bar, spoke to her, but her dark eyes were fixed on Janis.

Janis was sitting more or less across from her on a table with one thigh balanced on its edge, one black-and-white high-topped foot dangling and the other flat on the floor. She wore tight, faded blue denims and a loose white tank top that showed off her broad shoulders and tanned arms. Patty, one of the women sitting at the same table, said something to her, and Janis bent her head to listen. She grinned and sat up, tipping her glass for a couple of big swallows. As she wiped her mouth with the back of her hand, she looked up and noticed Carole watching her.

"Hey, Janis. Car okay?" Carole drawled, lifting her bottle in Janis's direction. "I thought maybe she was stalled when I passed you today."

"Carole." Janis raised her beer, too, and straightened up, half-sitting, half-standing, with both feet now planted on the floor. "Was that you in your grandmother's car?"

Their friends snickered and they both smiled, if a little thinly.

"You guys should have a race," Abby said.

Carole snorted. "Wanna shoot some pool?" she asked Janis. "The table's free." Janis had beaten her two out of three games a few nights back, and Carole wanted payback.

They moved to the pool table at the back of the room, set their beers on a nearby table, and took a couple of cues off the wall, examining them carefully. Some of the other women gathered around to watch. Janis shoved a few coins in the tray, pushed, and the balls came rumbling out into the slot under the end of the table. Carole loved that sound and always imagined a network of dark tunnels under the tabletop through which the colorful balls raced at breakneck speed. She racked them up, solid and striped, into the triangle for eight-ball.

The lamp above the table turned Janis's short feathered hair to copper as she bent forward, sighting down her cue to break. Her top gapped open, partially revealing the swell of her breasts to Carole at the other end of the table. Carole quickly shifted her eyes away, but not soon enough to prevent her stomach from clenching and her face from reddening, to her total and utter consternation.

After the balls finished breaking, sinking one, Janis pocketed one more. Carole was still rattled, her cheeks hot, when Janis winked and stared at her pointedly, waiting for her to shoot. She failed to make a ball, but finally did get it together, and the score was four games to three for her by the time the bartender announced, "Time, ladies," and they called it a night.

Carole lived nearby, so she walked home as she usually did after an evening of drinking. What the fuck *was* that! Her reaction to seeing Janis's cleavage—pulse quickening, guts buzzing, and *blushing* for god's sake!—had been a shock. She'd never been attracted to another butch, yet she'd actually been aroused. She must really need to get laid. That's all it was, she decided. But what was that wink? She shrugged it off.

As she turned into her driveway, she admired the massive old Lexus glowing softly silver in the dim light of the streetlamp. Seeing it reminded her of Abby's tongue-in-cheek suggestion and the reactions in the bar. The rumors had flown.

"Hey, Abby said you're gonna have a race. When?" Jude had asked, as if it were a *fait accompli.*

And, as Carole was racking the balls up once more, this from Cindy, who was very cute and one of Janis's exes: "Janis, can I drop the flag, pulleeze?"

Carole and Janis had mostly just grinned and brushed off the comments and questions and concentrated on their game. Their friends wouldn't let it go, though.

As Carole lay in bed going back over the evening, her thoughts lingered on the peculiar incident at the pool table. She drifted off in an erotic haze, her hand in Janis's shirt, reaching for a nipple. *No*! She came to with a start and sat up, heart racing. She breathed deeply to calm herself and then lay back down on her stomach and thrust her hand down, under her body, touching herself. She was *so* wet. She willed herself to think about somebody else, one of her current fantasies. She climbed on top of the gorgeous—and ultrafeminine—woman she'd been admiring at the gym, and took her hard, on a mat, pushing her fingers into her. Then she was licking her, all wet and hot, and the woman was writhing and moaning. In her imagination, even though Carole was going down on her, she was able to see the woman's face while she was coming. But as she jerked herself to a shuddering climax, the face dissolved into Janis's, and it was Janis arching against her and moaning with pleasure.

On Wednesdays—Hump Day—Red Emma's was usually pretty full right after work, as the women took advantage of the pub food served only on that day and on the weekend. That Wednesday was no exception. Carole and Abby were both sitting on bar stools eating and talking, occasionally glancing up at the mirror behind the bar to check out the room, when Abby said, "So what about that race, eh? C'mon, how about it? I'm serious. What a gas."

Carole shoveled a forkful of meat pie into her mouth, ignoring the question.

"You *know* you'd really like that SUV to eat your dust, not to mention its driver." Abby continued harassing her.

"Are you nuts? We'd get caught and they'd take away my car. Forget it." Nevertheless, she felt a tiny thrill, quickly suppressed.

Abby chewed thoughtfully. "No, you wouldn't—we wouldn't."

Carole regarded her best friend in the mirror. Uh-oh. Abby had the look that meant all the wheels were turning, and "no" would be a remote option when she finally marshaled her arguments.

Just at that moment, they saw Janis passing behind them. Abby whirled around and grabbed her arm, almost spilling the glass of beer in Janis's hand.

"Janis! C'mere. We're still talking about that race."

"No, we're not. I've been telling her no way," Carole growled. She hoped she sounded normal. Part of her mind was trying desperately not to think of her masturbatory fantasy of the other night.

"No way is right. We'd get caught and they'd take away my car," Janis said.

"What I said." Carole nodded solemnly.

"C'mon, Janis, you know you'd love to see that big old boat eat your dust," Abby urged. Indignantly Carole raised her eyebrows at her. "And I know just how you won't get caught." Abby smiled conspiratorially and lowered her voice. "You know my parents' farm north of town?"

Carole nodded. She'd been there many times.

"Well, it's huge, right?" Abby continued. "Lots of fields, mostly corn. Very tall corn. A couple of fields are fallow every summer, though. Just clover. You can see right across the field—no obstructions—so you could race around that. If there's one with cornfields all around, nobody would see us. And if it's at noon on a Sunday, nobody's around, anyway."

"What about the noise?" Carole asked, in spite of herself.

Janis just stared at them with round eyes.

"It's in the middle of nowhere, and nobody's gonna call the cops just because they hear a couple of engines revving."

"Are you guys nuts?" Janis found her voice. "I already said *no*!" She didn't sound as vehement as she might have, though.

"Hey, I haven't said *yes* either," Carole said.

But soon some of the others got involved in the discussion. They were all so high with enthusiasm that finally Carole and

Janis got caught up in the excitement, too, and caved and said yes. Red Emma's buzzed with anticipation all that evening.

One woman suggested taking bets. Jude quashed that idea pretty quickly. They could be in enough trouble already without adding illegal gambling to illegal racing.

"Listen up, everybody," Abby said in her take-charge, gravelly voice. "The race will be this Sunday. High noon. Do not advertise it, even as a joke. Don't talk about the race. If this gets back to us from outside this group, we'll have to cancel."

"But I was thinking of doing a poster for the bar. *Butch-on-Butch Street Racing,*" said Patty. Everybody laughed, but Abby glared at Patty. "Hey, I won't. I'm only kidding. Geez."

The butches in question both flushed as their glances locked. Neither seemed able to look away. Carole was dimly aware that Abby was watching them, fascinated, her eyes going from one to the other. Then somebody called to somebody else across the room, and the moment was over.

Carole's pulse was speeding. She could feel it in her throat. She refused to look at Abby as she passed by her to fetch a beer from the bar. Swallowing the cool liquid gratefully, she tried to slow down her breathing. Abby was at her side almost immediately.

"Hey, what's going on with you two?" she hissed.

"Nothing." Carole gave her a look that said, "Drop it or else," so Abby did, but she gave her a look in turn that said, "I don't believe you."

"Okay, so it's this Sunday, twelve o'clock," Abby said. "I'll find out where and look after all the details."

On Saturday morning Carole decided to check out the location of the pending race, maybe have a look at the road. She was familiar with the area and had no trouble finding the field

Abby had described. She drove around it once. It measured about three-quarters of a mile on each side, flat as a pancake like the rest of the surrounding countryside. A shallow ditch ran along both sides of the road. No telephone poles, though, and the road was wide and paved. It was gray and roughly surfaced with age—rough was okay. It was in good condition, with no major cracks or potholes. The shoulders were only about a foot wide, but hard and dry with not much gravel. It didn't look as if traction would be a problem.

She stopped the Lexus and got out. A blast of heat hit her after the air-conditioning, even though the sun wasn't high yet. It shone into her eyes and reflected from the pavement, making her squint. The air was still, not the slightest rustle in the tall, dark green corn across the road, and the only sound the searing buzz of cicadas. Carole wondered where they were since she couldn't see any trees. Well, except for one that didn't count anymore. In the distance, a bare skeleton of a once-mighty elm stood alone in the middle of the field. She hadn't seen one of those in years, as most of them had died and been cut down long ago. Other than that, the field was empty, just a rock here and there. Abby was right; you could easily see from one side of the field to the other.

And that's why she could see a car coming even before it turned the corner onto the road where she was standing. Her guts contracted. A black Lexus SUV, shining in the sun. Janis.

Janis pulled up behind Carole's car and rolled down the window. "Wow, hot." They smiled at each other tentatively. "Checking things out?"

"Yeah," Carole said. "The road looks pretty good. Good surface. There's a ditch all around, though, on both sides."

Janis got out, examined the ditch, and looked out across the bare field. As usual, she was wearing faded blue 501s and a tank top. Carole admired her tight behind. She knew Janis worked out, just as she did. They often saw each other at the gym and would surreptitiously compare their buff physiques, or at least Carole did. She was pretty sure Janis did, too. All part of the competition between them, of course. As Carole took in Janis's arms and shoulders, she suddenly felt even warmer and turned away, concentrating on the cornstalks across the road. She wiped her sweaty forehead with her arm, pushing back the damp brown curls, and with her other hand pulled her clammy muscle shirt high up on her back to get some air on her body. When she turned back, she caught Janis looking, her gaze fastened on Carole's bare skin, her lips parted. Their eyes met, and Carole had the same reaction again as at the pool table at Red Emma's.

A flash of scarlet broke their concentration when a red-winged blackbird landed on the fence in the cornfield.

"Well, I guess I've seen everything—uh, the road and all, so..." Carole cleared her throat and dug in a front pocket of her own faded Levis for her car keys.

"Okay, see you tomorrow. Should be fun," Janis said a little awkwardly and followed Carole to her car.

But as Carole reached for the door handle, she felt a hand clasping her bare upper arm. Shocked, she turned around, and they stared at each other for a split second before she was pushed backward against her car.

"I've been wanting to do this," Janis said hoarsely, grabbing her shoulders and shoving her leg between Carole's. Carole grunted with surprise, immediately aware of her wet crotch against the friction of Janis's thigh. Automatically she pushed her own thigh up against Janis's sex and, hands on Janis's ass, pulled her in harder. This was all wrong, but she didn't care. She was too turned on. Both women groaned when their lips and tongues came together, and Carole threw her head back and arched against Janis as Janis's hot wet mouth moved to her neck. The only sound besides their harsh breathing was the cicadas, but they didn't hear them.

When Janis wedged a hand between their bodies, fumbling with the buttons of Carole's fly, Carole suddenly came to her senses. "Un-uh," she said, and with a heave threw Janis off and switched positions. Janis laughed breathlessly as Carole pressed her back against the door with her whole body, rocking her thigh between Janis's as she moved her hips slowly back and forth. This time it was she who trailed her lips and tongue down Janis's throat toward the breasts she'd fantasized about.

"Oh god," Janis said, and then, "I've never done this before," as she reached once more for Carole's buttons. This time Carole let her and moved back just enough to undo Janis's at the same time. As she touched smooth warm skin, Carole realized that she'd never unfastened a woman's fly buttons before either. Her femme girlfriends didn't wear Levi's with buttons.

Carole reached down Janis's belly to slick, swollen flesh at the same time as she felt a hand sliding through her hair and between her own labia. She leaned one arm against the car to keep from collapsing against Janis, leaving just enough room for their stroking. By now they were both moaning. Again they found each other's mouths, and their tongues glided together in the same rhythm as their fingers. After only a few seconds, Carole felt the first flutter of her muscles tightening into orgasm. She thrust farther into Janis's wet heat, and Janis cried out as they both came.

Limp and sweaty and still breathing hard, they leaned against the car side by side, hanging on to the door handles. The sun beat down on them, reflecting from the metal. With trembling fingers, they each did up their own buttons. They didn't look at each other. When Carole got her strength back, she got into her car and looked up at Janis through the open window. Janis's disheveled hair was a corona with the light behind her.

"You know I'm going to beat you, don't you?"

Carole blinked at the sudden change of direction. Janis's face was in shadow so she couldn't see it very well, but she sounded serious.

"Really. And why are you so sure?"

"Because I'm a better driver and my car's a lot faster."

Carole laughed. "Don't try to psych me out. It won't work. Not after this."

As she drove away, she watched Janis in the rearview mirror just standing there, looking after her, hands in her back pockets. Carole's hand on the steering wheel was damp. It must smell like Janis's cunt. She resisted the temptation to find out, not wanting to be aroused again, and wondered what the hell was going on with them. It was the heat, and they were both between women and extremely horny. It could have happened to anyone. She flushed and cringed a little inside. But with another butch?

The next day, Sunday, was even hotter. By noon it was already ninety-five in the shade; the sun was a weight pressing down on them. A small crowd had gathered. Carole counted eight cars (including both Lexi), three motorbikes, one scooter, and a bicycle, all parked well away from the actual raceway, the road encircling the empty field.

"Okay, listen up," Abby yelled in her official voice, raising a hand high. Then she said something into a squawking walkie-talkie. Apparently the woman at the other end was in the middle of the field under the dead elm, an observer with binoculars.

"The race will start in twenty minutes at the drop of the traditional green flag. It will begin here." Abby pointed at a white line spray-painted across the road. "It will proceed counterclockwise around all four sides of the field and end here at the drop of a rainbow flag." Everybody cheered and whistled at that. "For safety's sake, stay off the racetrack and well clear of the starting line and the finish. Competitors, come here, please."

Carole and Janis shuffled up to her. "A coin toss will determine your position. Heads or tails?" The drivers mumbled their choice, and Abby tossed a shiny coin spinning up into the air.

"Carole in the gray Lexus gets the inside; Janis in the black Lexus gets the outside. Now shake hands, and may the best woman win." They shook, grinning sheepishly, their hands clammy from heat and nerves; more cheering and whistling from the crowd.

As they sat in position in their softly purring cars, waiting behind the start line, Carole and Janis looked at each other for a long moment through the half-open windows. What passed between them at that moment Carole couldn't interpret, but somehow it felt good. She suddenly relaxed and wasn't nervous anymore. She stared straight ahead, focusing on the road, thankful that the sun was directly above and wouldn't shine in their eyes.

Five minutes to go. About fifteen feet up ahead, on the cornfield side of the road, Cindy appeared in pink halter top and short-shorts. She stood facing them, legs wide apart, holding up in one hand, as high as she could reach, what appeared to be a fluorescent lime green thong—the green flag for the start. There was no time to laugh. Carole glanced at the clock on the dash. Her heart rate picked up. Two minutes to go. They both revved their engines. She reveled in the sound—*rrrrum, rrrrum.*

Down came the green thong! They were off! Cindy was just a smudge in the landscape as they passed her, tires squealing, smelling of burning rubber, clouds of dust and grit following in their wake.

Carole stomped on the gas pedal. 0–60 in 7.9 seconds said the specs. She'd never tested that. It felt like 5 G's, forcing her backward against the seat. The SUV's specs said 0–60 in 6.8 seconds; she'd looked it up. She glanced over: neck and neck, and halfway down the first stretch. Two-thirds of the way, her speedometer read almost ninety mph. She sat in a tunnel of sound, wind whipping by the half-open windows, tires eating up the road, engines roaring. She had to slow down with the first corner coming up. The black SUV was pulling ahead. It must be that 0–60 in 6.8 takeoff, still an advantage in the first straightaway.

As Carole slowed down to forty to take the corner, Janis was almost a car length ahead of her. Janis took it wide, increasing the distance by another half car length as she zoomed over to the inside, cutting the gray car off but allowing Carole just enough room to stay in control directly behind her. They picked up speed again going into the second stretch. Relentlessly, Carole closed the distance between them to a half car length and then, just before running up the black car's bumper, she moved over to the outside, still closing.

Again they were abreast, burning up the road at almost a hundred. It was the same situation as in the first stretch, but with positions reversed. This time the gray car moved ahead, so gradually that they seemed to be standing still, side by side. Carole wasn't aware of the blur of the passing cornfield on her right, only of the straight road ahead and the black car on her left, which disappeared from her peripheral vision as she pulled ahead. Nearing the second corner, Carole was leading by at least a car length. Time to slow down again. Like Janis before, she took the outside corner wide and then swooped across to the inside, cutting Janis off but not giving her quite as much room as Janis had allowed. Maybe Janis hadn't decelerated as much when cornering.

Carole accelerated again, rapidly picking up speed down the third straightaway. Elated, she glanced in the rearview and right-side mirrors, needing to know the black car's exact position. She saw only dust. Puzzled, she looked again, losing speed without thinking. She knew the dust wasn't thick enough to hide a car close behind her.

Where was Janis? Fear clutched at her chest. She took her foot off the gas pedal and stepped hard on the brake, still glancing in the rearview mirrors. The gray car fishtailed wildly as she slowed it down to do a U-ie with one twist of the steering wheel. Big as it was, the old Lexus could turn on a dime. Carole raced back the way she'd come, peering apprehensively through the dust, eyes scanning the road, back and forth. After what seemed like eternity, suddenly, through the dust cloud, she saw the black car up ahead on her right, lying angled on its driver's side along the edge of the ditch. One wheel was still turning slowly and the front passenger-side door was sprung open.

"Oh, god, oh, god, no!" Carole's heart began to pound with dread. She skidded to a stop beside the SUV and jumped out. The car was about six feet wide, a little high to climb into from a ditch, especially if you added in having to climb over the seat, so she crawled frantically up the side of the hood to the open passenger door. She stuck her head in. Janis sat there, still buckled into her seat. But of course she wasn't actually sitting; she was lying on her side, on an air bag. A side air bag. Her eyes were closed, and she was making little groaning sounds.

"Janis! Janis! Are you okay? Are you okay? Oh god..." Carole's voice was hoarse and shaky.

"Not fucking okay...went into the ditch...you fucking cut me...off...oh shit," Janis muttered, and groaned again, eyes still closed.

"Look at me! Can you move? Can you turn your head? Please

open your eyes!" Carole was almost crying. Bending from the waist, she let herself down farther into the interior, anchored by her lower torso and legs outside the car. Distractedly, she heard a motorcycle pull up outside, then the squawk of the walkie-talkie and Abby's voice, but from her position she couldn't see anyone.

"Carole! Is Janis hurt?"

"I don't know! Call an ambulance! Janis!" Carole reached down to touch her shoulder. "Please look at me!"

Slowly Janis turned her head and opened her eyes to look at Carole. "See...can move my head," she croaked. At the sight of the familiar blue eyes, Carole's filled up, and a couple of drops fell down onto Janis's shoulder.

"Can you move your arms and legs?"

Janis moved the arm closest to Carole. "Other stuck..." Her left arm was imprisoned between her body and the air bag she was lying on. But she wiggled both hands and feet.

"Does anything hurt?" Carole managed to unbuckle the seat belt. Gravity pulled it down to fall on the air bag.

Janis didn't answer right away, as if she were checking for aches and pains. "Not...much...'m okay. Get me out."

Janis turned her upper body toward Carole, and Carole grasped her shoulders. Janis reached up her right arm and grabbed the outside edge of the passenger seat, and together they managed to pull her up enough so that she was kneeling on the air bag. They paused to get their breath, and Janis tested her left arm. "Hurts. I think it's broken." She spoke slowly but normally.

All that gym work paid off. They were both strong women and, with some help from Carole, and from Abby waiting outside, Janis was able to climb out of the car and down. But when they were back on the ground, she collapsed on a dusty strip of grass beside the ditch, moaning a little, her face white. "Arm hurts like fuck."

Carole sat and gathered her in her arms, cradling her head and shoulders against her chest as Janis closed her eyes and seemed to pass out.

Carole looked up at Abby. "It's all my fault. It's my fault. She could have died," she sobbed, as more tears tracked her grimy face.

Abby bent down and patted Carole's head sympathetically. "I don't know exactly what happened here, hon," she said soothingly. "We didn't see it up close, but she'll be okay. She's in shock. We've called an ambulance. We'll get her checked out." She moved away, and spoke into the walkie-talkie again. Carole heard her say, "She's okay."

By this time some of the others had gathered at the accident scene. They regarded the two women curiously, but discreetly kept their distance. Carole took no notice. Hardly knowing what she was doing, she buried her face in Janis's neck.

"Hey, it's okay," Janis whispered in her ear. "I'm okay, just tired." Her good arm came around Carole's neck, pulling her closer.

"I almost lost you."

"I'm not going anywhere." Carole could feel her smiling. She pulled away slightly, looking into Janis's face. Janis's eyes were clear.

"I'm so sorry. It's all my fault. I cut you off." Carole's eyes started tearing up again.

"Maybe. But I didn't slow down enough around that corner. When you passed me, I couldn't control the car and she went across the road, heading for the cornfield ditch. I yanked the wheel and she went for the other ditch, too fast to straighten out. She slid on her side along the ditch forever. That was scary."

Janis shuddered "I bet the grass in the ditch is all flattened out."

Carole looked. Indeed it was, flat for maybe forty feet.

"Good thing about the side bag," Janis continued, rambling a little. "Sure scared the hell out of me when that exploded. Probably broke my arm. Better than my head. Is my car okay?"

"I think it's fine. The side might need a paint job. We'll get the wrecker to pull her out. I'll call them after the ambulance picks you up, then find you at the hospital."

"Good," Janis said. "I'm so tired." She pulled Carole close again and closed her eyes.

In the distance they could hear the faint wail of a siren. Abby's walkie-talkie squawked again.

"Attention, please," she called out to the women milling about. "Here comes the ambulance, so before it gets here you'd better all leave, in the opposite direction. This was just an ordinary traffic accident, right? We'll all meet at Red Emma's later."

The women dispersed quickly. As the last few were leaving, Carole heard one of them say in a shocked voice, "Carole and Janis? Are you kidding me? Those two butches? No way!"

Way.

FLANNEL AND FLEECE

Cheyenne Blue

I'm not leaving you for another woman," my husband said. "I'm leaving you before you leave me for another woman."

I forced a smile. "Don't be ridiculous."

His answering smile was sad. "Jude, I've seen how you watch women, and you're not checking out their clothes. It's obvious you no longer love me. When was the last time we made love? Three, four months ago?

"I've got a job in the Texas oilfields. You can keep the house." He leaned forward and kissed me gently. "See you around, babe."

I live in a mountain town in Colorado. It's small, becoming trendy. The people are a mix of those who have been here forever, and those who have recently arrived, attracted by the outdoor lifestyle.

The newcomers are organic-food-eating, nonsmoking, holistically inclined, whitewater-rafting, snowboarding fitness freaks with children called Phoebe and Jacob. They drive SUVs with

Australian shepherds wearing bandanas sitting in the back. In summer they wear baggy cotton shorts and Tevas. In winter they wear fleece and Levi's. I call them fleeces.

Those who have been here forever are BBQ-eating, Republican-voting, elk-hunting, Coors-drinking, walking heart attacks with children called Wayne and Jolene. They drive dual-cab pickups with gun racks in the back. In summer they wear flannel shirts and Wranglers. In winter they wear flannel shirts and Wranglers. I call them flannels.

We are all such stereotypes.

People rallied around after Tom left. The women's cooperative gave me a "hardship discount" and told me I was lucky I didn't have kids to cramp my development as an independent woman. The flannel neighbors brought around casseroles and said they were so sorry I hadn't been blessed with children as they would have been a comfort and a reason to go on.

Really, both extremes were enough to make my eyes roll so fast it was a wonder they weren't spinning down the sidewalk and into the river.

I got a job as a care assistant in the medical center. I went hiking with the women's group. I was invited (not for the first time) to join two different congregations, and (not for the last time) I politely refused. Because I was a fleece, I drank in Colby's, where the happy hour margaritas were big and icy and they allowed dogs on the patio. The flannel crowd drank happy hour pints of Coors Light in the dimness of the Doubleheader Saloon. Both crowds rubbed along amicably in the Mountain Pearl, where the long wooden bar jostled fleece and flannel elbows and the pressed-tin ceilings were high enough that any differences evaporated into the air-conditioning.

I got asked out now that I was an unattached woman. I

turned down most of the offers, although I had a few dates with a river guide and a one-night stand with the guy who ran the computer store in town.

Tom's words often ran through my head, and if I ever caught myself staring at a woman I'd divert my gaze. I wasn't ready to go there. It wasn't that I had a problem with lesbians; it was just that I didn't see myself in that basket. After all, I'd been married. I slept with men. I thought that was how my wiring ran.

There was just one problem. Everywhere I went in town, I kept bumping into Jan.

I'd seen her around before; she was kind of hard to miss. She stood six feet tall in work boots, and cropped brown hair with wings of gray hugged her head. She was a rawboned woman; the sort who never looks slender, even though she didn't carry an ounce of surplus on her frame. She usually drank in the Doubleheader, but I'd seen her in the grocery store, driving her pickup around town, buying smokes, and sitting in the park staring at the river. She was definitely a flannel.

After Tom left, she was quite literally everywhere I went. I dropped in for after-work drinks in the Mountain Pearl with the hospital crew and Jan was there, her back to the bar, sipping her Coors and watching me with an amused look as I played pool. I was buying veggies in the co-op, and I literally bumped into her studying the shiitake and oyster mushrooms in bewilderment. My hip tingled from the contact with her rangy frame.

"Sorry," I muttered.

She didn't answer, but I could feel her eyes following me as I wheeled my cart around into the coffee aisle.

She even turned up on a Saturday hike with the women's group, as out of place as a pit bull in a pack of poodles. Her flannel shirt was worn and comfortable, rolled up to show strong, sinewy arms, and her Wranglers brushed the top of a pair of leather work boots. Jan hiked in silence, always a little behind me. I could feel her eyes on my butt, and my breath hopped faster with the implications. We hiked among the aspens, golden in the crisp fall day, until we climbed above the tree line and the day was bright and sharp and the land spread beneath us. The other women chattered among themselves; Jan and I stood silent, taking in the view, united in our separateness.

People noticed, of course. Marcia in the co-op told me a story of a girlfriend she'd had at college. One of the church ladies dropped around to try and recruit me and said that by coming along to their prayer meetings I could arrest my descent into sin.

"What descent?" I asked.

The church lady spluttered a bit. "You're all alone," she said, "and we don't want the wrong sort of people to take notice of you. God says that a man and a woman should be together."

I showed her the door, and she didn't return. It meant I didn't get any more casseroles, but I was getting sick of Betty Crocker anyway.

Jan's silent campaign was having an effect. I began to look out for her, and although I still ignored her, I began to let myself think. Did I find her attractive? Could I see myself in her bed?

Oh yes.

I started to dream about what she would look like naked. She'd have jutting hip bones, with hollows you could put your fist in. Her stomach would be flat and hard, but I'd be able to rest my cheek on it and feel her pulse underneath my skin and smell her musk below my nose. I could trace the veins in her arms and entangle her lean, strong legs in mine until she rolled me underneath her and kissed me and we began to love all over again.

Two months after I first noticed her following me, I walked into Colby's on a Friday and saw her there at the bar. Instead of a Coors, she had a frosted salt-crusted margarita in front of her.

I hesitated. Did I want to do this?

Yes.

What was I worried about?

Nothing.

Taking a deep breath, I walked over and slid onto the stool next to her.

"Thought you were more the beer-drinking type," I said.

She turned to me, and her eyes crinkled at the corners. "I'm on a mission. If drinking margaritas is what it takes, then I'll put up with this lime shit." She signaled the barman. "What will you have?"

"Coors Light for me."

Her mouth quirked up, and the barman slapped a frosted pint in front of me. I hate Coors-friggin'-Light. It tastes of horse piss. Diluted horse piss at that. I drank half of it in one go, grimacing at the taste.

"Here," she said, and swapped my glass for hers. Deliberately, she set her lips where mine had been on the glass and drank.

The salt was only missing from the glass where her lips had been. I turned on my stool and let my eyes roam her body. "So, gonna tell me why you're following me?"

"If you don't know that, then you're denser than a mountain pine forest."

"I have a husband."

"Don't look like he's around much anymore."

"You probably vote Republican."

She hooted. "You don't know me at all, do you?"

"I'm straight."

"And I'm Bette Davis."

I set my lips to her glass, tasting the salt and the sour and the lime. "Now what?"

She swiveled around to face me, and her hands came down on my thighs. I felt each imprint of her finger, tiny little pads of heat burning through my jeans.

"I want you, Jude. And I think you want me. Am I right?"

I stared back at her, seeing her earnest expression, so different from the laconic amusement she normally wore as easily as her flannel shirt. Her fingers twitched once on my leg, and that betrayal of her doubt gave me my final answer.

"Yes," I breathed. "Yes, I want you."

Without another word she stood, and taking my hand, led me out of the bar, past my friends and workmates drinking margaritas in the corner, past the groups of pool-playing women from the co-op. Her truck was outside. She hopped up and opened the door for me.

She didn't say where she was going; I'd assumed her place or mine, but she took the highway out of town before turning off onto the county road. The pickup bounced over the washboard surface. I propped my chin on my hand and stared out of the passenger window, at the aspens, golden in the purple dusk; at the horses picking over the yellowed grass; at the way the Rockies shone clean with fresh snow. It meant I didn't have to look at Jan. I wasn't sure I could; I wasn't sure I could take the knowledge and confidence in her eyes. Yes, my decision was made and there was no going back, but I wasn't sure I could stare it straight in the eye. Not just yet, anyway.

Jan turned onto a Jeep trail that led steadily up the range, and then another smaller trail, before the pickup came to a stop at a sparse campsite. There were the remains of a campfire, a couple of discarded cans, and a small tent, pitched in the half shelter of a juniper. I got out and walked over to the lip where the ground dropped away down to the valley. On the far side, the Collegiate Peaks rose as sharp as a bleach stain against the dark cloth of the sky. A single bright star shone through the weave, a lone beacon, and the aspens quaked in a brief evening breeze.

Jan was behind me, dragging a cooler out of the pickup's tray and carting it over to the tent. She knelt, and for a moment I saw her taut butt as she worked the zipper. Then she was inside, boots left at the door and the fly of the tent tied back to let in the night.

"What are you waiting for?"

I ducked down and entered, shucking my boots at the entrance as she had done, falling forward onto sleeping bags spread out over a foam mattress. Jan reclined, beer in hand, so that she could see out the door. I wondered how she'd managed it so fast.

She put the beer down and held out her arms. "Come here."

I moved into her arms as if I'd settled there every night for the last several millennia, with my head on her breast and my hand curved around her waist. She held me close, her free hand stroking my hair, and we breathed in unison, soft, slurry breaths that sucked in the frosted air. I was lightheaded from her closeness. *This* was the unspoken wanting that I'd barely acknowledged even to myself. *This* was why Tom had left me. *This* was where I wanted to be.

The rightness of it seeped slowly through my skin, infusing my body like a shot of bourbon. I raised my head to look at her.

"Jan?" I whispered.

Her face was soft, relaxed in the dimness of the tent. Her hand wound itself into my hair, as if she were afraid I was sliding away from her.

"I think you should kiss me."

Lean brown hands raised me from her body, supporting me

upright, so that I was forced to straddle her for balance. I stared down at her glittering eyes, the slight breasts barely peaking the soft flannel shirt.

"If you want me, you better kiss me," she said.

I didn't hesitate. Bending, I fitted my lips to hers, an unexpected softness in such a hard body. Her hips bucked underneath my weight, settling me more firmly in place. My hair fell over her face as we kissed, and she made a funny little noise in the back of her throat, a hum of satisfaction as it tickled her cheek. And still we kissed. She kissed softly for such a hard woman. She was all heat and sucking moisture, and her lips moved with assurance, giving me no chance to retreat back to a place she couldn't reach. Her tongue danced lightly around my mouth, until I felt there was no place left untasted.

Finally, when my breath was sobbing in my throat, I pulled back. Her eyes were wide and dark in the dim light, and a half smile crooked her mouth.

My body pulsated where it rested on her jeans. "Show me more," I breathed.

Jan reared up and her strong hands twisted themselves in my hair, anchoring me to her. The softness was gone. In its place was a fierce glittering possession. It was there in her kiss that sucked the breath out of my body, it was there in the anchoring of her hands on my head, it was there in the way her hips bucked, grinding into my crotch. Our tongues danced, and the thought of hers on other, more intimate parts of my body made me shudder in anticipation.

Jan broke the kiss, and her fingers moved to the buttons of my shirt, shucking them in turn and then pushing the material down from my shoulders. The cool air licked my skin, raising goose bumps. Her fingers trailed down to the upper swell of my breasts, tracing the line where the edge of white lace touched my skin. Her face was intent, a half smile of discovery, and her fingers moved like water over my flesh. Bending, she followed the path of her eyes with her mouth. I shuddered with the heat of her tongue and its wet, hot glide.

Her breath warmed my nipple through the lace bra, hot damp moisture bathing its peak. Jan reached behind and unsnapped it, pulling the straps from my shoulders. Her mouth lifted long enough for the bra to fall away, discarded between us. Now her lips caressed my bare flesh, teething and tonguing my nipple to a white-hot stiffness.

With an abrupt motion, she rolled me over, so that my back pressed into the soft cotton sleeping bags. Jan was now on top, and her fingers worked the snap of my jeans with an urgency I hadn't experienced since high school. The buttons fell open, and her fingers delved down, drumming on my stomach before moving insistently lower. They hesitated for a second at the top of my panties—lace, like my bra—before moving firmly down, brushing through my curls, down lower, to where I needed her to be.

A finger settled firmly on my clit. "It's not just about you," she said.

In turn, I flicked the buttons of her shirt. She didn't wear a bra, and her breasts were mere swells from her chest bone. My fingers brushed her nipples—so strange to touch a woman so freely; so magical, so *right*—and I watched, fascinated, as they peaked underneath my touch.

Jan's finger moved in circles around my clit. "Is this what you like?" Her voice was soft in the enclosure of her tent. "Would you like my mouth here?"

"Oh yes," I breathed, imagining the way her tongue would move over my cunt. My fingers rubbed her nipples, a firmer touch when she shuddered.

She rolled to one side and tugged at my jeans. I lifted my hips to assist, and the cool air licked my exposed skin. Jan tossed aside my panties, jeans, and socks, and then shed her own. Naked, she returned to me, pushing apart my knees, rolling onto her stomach between my parted thighs.

My breath came in short gasps. I've always felt uncomfortable, having a man staring at my exposed pussy, uneasy with the ownership in his gaze. But Jan's gaze licked over my cunt, and her breath grazed my inner thighs. I felt her avarice, I felt her delight.

Her breath scorched my flesh, and she moved forward until I could feel her moist panting on my sex. Then her face was between my thighs and her tongue touched me lightly, withdrew, then returned, firmer, harder, friction and suction and heat and light, all concentrated between my thighs. In the dimness of the tent, my eyes closed and my hands moved down to grip tightly around Jan's head.

She knew her way around a woman's pussy. Her tongue circled, flicked over the hood, and then settled into long, flat strokes that had me grasping her head and howling into the cool mountain night. The climax built in a crescendo of feeling, and my thighs clenched around her ears, hips rising from the sleeping bag. Still Jan didn't ease up as I hovered there on the brink; her tongue stroked and licked, her face so firmly between my legs I wondered how she could breathe. And then finally, the hot, wet press of her tongue pushed me over the edge, and I came in great gulps of air, my pussy pushed on her face.

Afterward, Jan stayed between my legs, stroking my inner thighs, her lips occasionally pressing to my cunt. But I knew there was more to my initiation than this. So I aligned myself with her body, rolling her onto her side, wrapping a leg over her hips. My fingers walked down her stomach to press into her wet cleft. I watched her face as my fingers slipped in and out, moving easily in her moisture. Her eyes were wide open, darting over my face, as if she were afraid of what she would see.

"It's okay," I soothed. "I'm here. I'm not going anywhere." And she sighed, and relaxed, and my fingers followed pathways familiar and new, sliding over anatomy that was not my own, learning the motions that gave her pleasure, until her thighs clenched around my hand and her breath was staccato on my face.

We slept that night wrapped tightly in each other's arms. In the morning, I woke to find the tent flaps pulled back and the low fall morning spilling in the door. Jan was already up, and the smell of coffee wafted back to me. Donning a shirt and boots, I crawled out to join her. She was fully dressed, her face tight and wary. Wrapping my arms around her waist, I rested my face against her shoulder.

"Morning, lover," I said.

Her breath sighed in my hair, and she tilted my face up to hers.

Tom came back from Texas, leaner and browner, his face questioning. I let him in, and he shared coffee with me. When Jan appeared from the bedroom, long strong legs bare beneath her flannel shirt, Tom nodded once, a short jerk of acknowledgment.

"I'll leave you to it," he said. "See you around, Jude."

Rising from the table, he bent to kiss me. His thin lips brushed over mine, and then he was gone, striding out into the bright day.

I met Jan's eyes over the dirty coffee mugs, and she reached over and entwined my hand in hers. I clasped it tightly, and smiled out into the sunlight.

ABOUT THE AUTHORS

JACQUELINE APPLEBEE's (writing-in-shadows.co.uk) stories have appeared in various anthologies and websites, including Clean Sheets; *Iridescence: Sensuous Shades of Lesbian Erotica; Best Women's Erotica 2008;* and *Best Lesbian Erotica 2008*. She is also the author of the paranormal novella *Fallen Soldiers*.

CHEYENNE BLUE has published stories in many anthologies, including *Best Women's Erotica; Best Lesbian Love Stories; Rode Hard, Put Away Wet;* and *Mammoth Book of Lesbian Erotica*. She moves between Australia, Ireland, and Colorado.

MAGGIE CEE (thefemmeshow.com) is the founder and artistic director of The Femme Show, showcasing femme visibility and queer art for queer people. She has been a guest artist with Body Heat: Femme Porn Tour, at Dixon Place's Hot! Festival, and the Femme2008 conference.

CHARLOTTE DARE (myspace.com/charlotte_dare) has published erotic fiction in *Tales of Travelrotica for Lesbians, Vol. 2; Ultimate Lesbian Erotica 2008* and *2009; Wetter; Purple Panties; Island Girls;* and *Where the Girls Are: Urban Lesbian Erotica.*

DANIELLE DE SANTIAGO (desantiago@gmx.de) is a French-Brazilian writer who lives in Germany and commutes between Aachen and Berlin. "I've Been Around the Block..." is dedicated to Trix Niederhauser.

SHAIN EVERETT juggles the demands of her writing, her day job, and a tow-headed little boy that calls her Mama. "The Oldest Virgin" marks her own deflowering; it is the first erotic story she has ever written.

SCARLETT FRENCH is a short-story writer and a poet. Her erotic fiction has appeared in *Best Women's Erotica 2009, Tasting Him: Oral Sex Stories; Lipstick on Her Collar; Best Women's Erotica 2008; Fantasy: Untrue Stories of Lesbian Passion; Best Women's Erotica 2007; Tales of Travelrotica for Lesbians; First Timers: True Stories of Lesbian Awakening; Best Lesbian Erotica 2005;* and *Va Va Voom.* She lives in London.

D. L. KING (dlkingerotica.com) is the publisher and editor of the review site Erotica Revealed, and the editor of the anthology *Where the Girls Are: Urban Lesbian Erotica.* She has published two novels, *The Melinoe Project* and *The Art of Melinoe,* as ebooks. Some of her latest short stories can be found in the anthologies *Best Lesbian Erotica 2008; Yes, Sir: Erotic Stories of Female Submission; Yes, Ma'am: Erotic Stories of Male Submission; Frenzy: 60 Stories of Sudden Sex; Mammoth Book of Best New Erotica 2008; Best Women's Erotica 2009;* and *Swing!*

Adventures in Swinging by Today's Top Erotica Authors.

CATHERINE LUNDOFF (visi.com/~clundoff) is an award-winning author and editor whose stories have appeared in more than sixty publications. She is the author of two collections of lesbian erotica: 2008 Goldie winner *Crave: Tales of Lust, Love, and Longing; Night's Kiss;* and editor of the fantasy and horror anthology *Haunted Hearths and Sapphic Shades: Lesbian Ghost Stories* (all Lethe Press). She lives in Minneapolis.

SOMMER MARSDEN (SmutGirl.blogspot.com) has written stories for dozens of anthologies, including *I Is for Indecent; J Is for Jealousy; L Is for Leather; Spank Me; Tie Me Up; Whip Me; Ultimate Lesbian Erotica 2008; Love at First Sting; Open for Business; Tasting Her;* and *Yes, Sir.* She lives in Maryland.

KRISTEN MONROE (aphrodites-table.blogspot.com) has written erotic fiction for Clean Sheets, Erotic Woman, Sexual Fiction, and other websites.

JEAN ROBERTA (JeanRoberta.com) teaches English in a Canadian prairie university and writes in various genres. Her erotic stories have appeared in over 60 print anthologies, including seven editions of the annual *Best Lesbian Erotica* series and her single-author collection, *Obsession* (Eternal Press). She writes reviews for the website eroticarevealed.com and a monthly column, "Sex is All Metaphors," for erotica-readers.com.

KYLE SONTZ is a twenty-four-year-old bookstore clerk who lives in Brooklyn and occasionally writes. He hopes to eventually be a writer who lives in Brooklyn, who occasionally works in a bookstore.

RENÉE STRIDER has published fiction in the *Erotic Interludes* series, volumes 2-5 (Bold Strokes), *Fantasy* (Bella), *Read These Lips* (RTL), *Best Lesbian Love Stories: Summer Flings* (Alyson); and *Toe to Toe* (Bedazzled Ink). She has lived throughout the United States and in the Netherlands, and now resides in Canada.

FRAN WALKER (franwalker@ihug.co.nz) has recently published short fiction in the online magazine Khimairal Ink (October 2008) and in the anthologies *Read These Lips 2* and *Chilling Tales*. She lives with her spouse, the novelist L-J Baker, in New Zealand.

ANNA WATSON has published short stories in various anthologies, including *Best Lesbian Erotica 2007, 2008,* and *2009; Fantasy: Untrue Stories of Lesbian Passion;* and Suspect Thoughts' anthology on drag kings (forthcoming). She writes for Custom Erotica Source as Cate Shea.

KRISTINA WRIGHT (kristinawright.com) is an award-winning writer whose erotic stories have appeared in more than fifty anthologies, including *Dirty Girls: Erotica for Women; Bedding Down: A Collection of Winter Erotica; Lipstick on Her Collar;* and four editions of *Best Lesbian Erotica*. She lives in suburban Virginia.

LUX ZAKARI (myspace.com/luxzakari) has written erotica for the websites Oysters & Chocolate and Clean Sheets. She is working on an erotic novel about the 1970s.

ABOUT THE EDITOR

SACCHI GREEN lives and writes in western Massachusetts and the mountains of New Hampshire, with occasional tours of the real world. Her stories have appeared in a hip-high stack of books with inspirational covers, including seven volumes of *Best Lesbian Erotica*, four of *Best Women's Erotica, Best Lesbian Romance 09, Zaftig, Best S/M Erotica 2, Penthouse* and *The Mammoth Book of Best New Erotica*. She has also coedited three lesbian erotica anthologies, *Rode Hard, Put Away Wet; Hard Road, Easy Riding* and *Lipstick on Her Collar*. Online, she can be found at http://sacchig.livejournal.com.